COMPANY
K

The Library of Alabama Classics,

reprint editions of works important

to the history, literature, and culture of

Alabama, is dedicated to the memory of

Rucker Agee

whose pioneering work in the fields

of Alabama history and historical geography

continues to be the standard of

scholarly achievement.

COMPANY

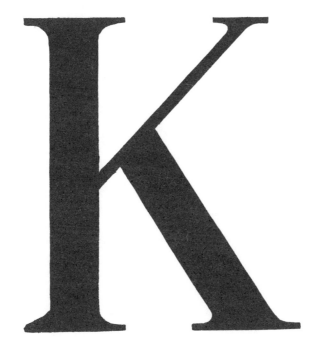

K

BY WILLIAM MARCH

With an Introduction by
Philip D. Beidler

The University of Alabama Press
Tuscaloosa

Introduction Copyright © 1989 by
The University of Alabama Press
Tuscaloosa, Alabama 35487–0380
All rights reserved
Manufactured in the United States of America

∞

The paper on which this book is printed meets the minimum
requirements of American National Standard for Information
Science-Permanence of Paper for Printed Library Materials,
ANSI A39.48-1984.

Library of Congress Cataloging-in-Publication Data

March, William, 1893-1954.
        Company K / William March : with an introduction by
    Philip D. Beidler.
            p.   cm. — (Library of Alabama classics)
        Includes bibliographical references.
        ISBN 0-8173-0480-0 (alk. paper)
            1. World War,—1914–1918—Fiction.   I. Title. II. Series.
    PS3505.A53157C6   1989   89–38395
    813'.54—dc20   CIP

British Library Cataloguing-in-Publication Data available

CONTENTS

INTRODUCTION
Philip D. Beidler

The Text of *Company K*

IN its simple physical presence, the revised final typescript of William March's *Company K* in the University of Alabama Special Collections Library speaks silently, yet movingly, of the cost of struggle it must have exacted upon the man who wrote it. The cover is a reinforced brown binder, of the sort available in any business supply or stationery shop. On the front, neatly traced out in ink—the sort of thing someone can do carefully with a pen and a ruler—is a small frame design, a rectangle-within-a-rectangle pattern looking faintly art-deco. Within the rectangle, again very neatly traced out in ink, are two lines of bold, yet simple lettering: the top one reads, COMPANY K; and the one just below it, WILLIAM MARCH.

After two blank pages of good quality bond, we come across the first printing, from a sound typewriter of clear, even impression. The ribbon ink is blue. Today the text is faded sufficiently to be mistaken for carbon copy; looking closely, however, one sees that it is clearly original. In the upper left corner, we read:

William March
Apartment 16-G
302 West 12th St.
New York, N.Y.

INTRODUCTION

Below, centered on the page and underlined, is once again the title: *Company K*.

There follows a dedication page, which reads: "To Ed Roberts, An Unchanging Friend." We then move immediately into the first narrative. In the published text, it is headed, as are all the chapters, by the name of the individual narrator, who is "Private Joseph Delaney"; but here, in the typescript, there is no such heading. We simply begin to read: "We have had supper and my wife and I are sitting on the porch."

The narrator of the section, we also quickly find out, happens to be the "author" of the book. He wonders what he has accomplished. He has wanted it to be not just about his company of men in war but about any company of men in any war, about nothing less than war itself. His wife observes that he might do well to omit the part, at least, about the shooting of the prisoners. She also ventures a theory about the way nature seems to concentrate special powers of regeneration upon the landscape of old battlefields. "Delaney," as we will come to know him only in the published text, disagrees. "To me," he concludes, "it has always seemed that God is so sickened with men, and their unending cruelty to each other, that he covers the places where they have been as quickly as possible."

If one looks at the pagination of the typescript as one reads this opening section, one observes that the omission of Delaney's name was probably not accidental. The four pages in question are lettered, not numbered. They are pages A, B, C, and D. The typescript then takes up the other individual narratives of which the text is composed. Each is headed by the narrator's name. The pages are numbered consecutively, from 1 to 198.

INTRODUCTION

The chief impression one gets of all this is of decision and control. Everything seems to be in its place: binding, lettering, arranging, dedicating, entitling—and in the first instance, not entitling—paginating. It all strikes us as quite calm and businesslike—this text of the most furious novel of war ever written by an American up to its time and quite arguably at least as furious and graphic as any written since. And therein lies a great part of the story. (By curious coincidence, the final manuscript of its only predecessor to make any comparable claim to unflinching naturalistic honesty, *The Red Badge of Courage*, may be seen at the University of Virginia library in a comparably businesslike draft, where, in the early pages, one may see neatly crossed out names such as "Fleming," "Wilson," and "Conklin," and neatly substituted generic phrases such as "the youth," "the loud soldier," "the tall soldier," and the like.) Control, one senses, must have been enacted at an enormous price. And the story of how *Company K* came to be turns out to be just this: that for William March in particular the price came awfully high.

William March and *Company K*

THE biographical circumstances of the genesis of *Company K* are likewise attended with a similar strange sense of quiet, impervious enigma. We do know for certain that William Edward Campbell, to be remembered by the literary world as William March, was born in Mobile in September 1893 and experienced a fairly typical southern childhood of the period in the small towns of Alabama and the Florida Panhandle. We know that after some study of law in the early years of this century at the University of Alabama and later at Valparaiso University in Indiana, and after a clerkship in law in New York City, March enlisted in the U.S. Marine Corps and saw action in some of its hardest campaigning in World War I in France. We likewise know for a fact that as a result of his actions specifically during an assault on Blanc Mont, March received the French Croix de Guerre and *both* the Distinguished Service Cross and the Navy Cross for valor. (The latter feat, one should add, to anyone with a knowledge of the military services, is literally mind-defying. The two decorations constitute the second highest awards, next only to the Congressional Medal of Honor, of what were then the two main branches of the American armed forces, the Army and the Navy.) We know that after the war he became an organizer and later vice-president of the Waterman Steamship Corporation, and then moved for an extended period to New York, where, eventually resigning the successful business position that also carried him abroad in the 1930s to such places as Hamburg and London, he became the author of *Company K*, of a large body of short stories including some of the most remarkable of his exceedingly talented American generation, and of several other novels, including most notably *Come in at the Door*, *The Tallons*, and *The Looking Glass*. We know that near the end of his life, he returned home to the South where, in a quiet house in the French Quarter of New Orleans, he composed his last book, *The Bad Seed*—ironically, as it became transmuted after his death first into a play and later into movie form, a work of a kind of semi-notoriety he would have found concomitantly amusing and faintly distasteful—and eventually died in his sleep one night in mid-May 1954.

INTRODUCTION

Of what happened to William Edward Campbell in France that specifically made him William March, the author of *Company K*, we have a general record. A member of the Fifth Marines in the United States Second Division, March saw his first action on the old Verdun battlefield near Les Eparges and shortly afterward at Belleau Wood, where he was wounded in the head and shoulder. He returned in time for Saint-Mihiel and for the attack on Blanc Mont, where he performed so extraordinarily as to receive the three major decorations for valor cited above. He then participated in the Meuse-Argonne and, along with his company, was preparing for a new assault crossing of the Meuse itself at Mouzon when the war ended.

In addition to this summary view, we also have the more focused and suggestive record of March's own after-the-fact reminiscences and pronouncements, and particularly of his going back in conversation on repeated occasions, we discover, to a critical episode—one, it seems, in which while isolated from his company, he encountered face to face, a German youth, blond and blue-eyed, at whom he instinctively lunged with his bayonet. As Roy S. Simmonds, March's biographer, describes the rest of the incident, the young German "stumbled and the bayonet pierced his throat, killing him instantly, his eyes wide open and staring into William's face" (23). In this same connection, we also must adduce some few further facts of subsequent psychological history, particularly in light of what a current American generation of war now again attempts to come to terms with under the weighty clinical designation of "post-traumatic stress." Again, Simmonds puts it succinctly: "It is certainly not without significance that at various stages of his life March experienced hysterical conditions related to both his throat and eyes" (23).

Of information concerning the specific episode of bravery that won William March that chestful of medals, we have curiously little. Available to us at least, is the citation to the Croix de Guerre, which reads: "During the operations in Blanc Mont region, October 3rd–4th, 1918, he left a shelter to rescue the wounded. On October 5th, during a counter-attack, the enemy having advanced to within 300 meters of the first aid station, he immediately entered the engagement and though wounded refused to be evacuated until the Germans were thrown back."

We have also the citations for the Distinguished Service and Navy Crosses, but they too are notably scant on particular information. We must simply know of William March's bravery, in the main, that he surely had it. And even without what we have of the biographical record or the medals or the certificates, of course, we would still know that he had it. It would still be there, inscribed in *Company K*, in a novel by a man who had clearly been to war, who had clearly seen his share of the worst of it, who had somehow survived, and who had committed himself afterward to the new bravery of sense-making embodied in the creation of major literary art. It is of that bravery that we still have the record of magnificent achievement, the brave and terrible gift of *Company K*.

Context and Prophecy:
Company K and the American Literature of War

The history of the place of *Company K* in the tradition of American writing about war is at least to date a curious one.

INTRODUCTION

When it came upon the scene, it was in large measure un-precedented in a literature of battle that had been oddly reticent about its actualities. Out of print for some time until being returned to publication, it now sits before us in the peculiar strangeness of the neglected cult classic. The story that lies between is at once one of a book that effectively inscribed a literary context and in the process became the stuff of literary prophecy.

Our nation is, after all, a nation born of war. It is also one that in 1861–65 passed through the most cataclysmic episode of mass fratricide known to history. One finds it curious, therefore, that its realistic fiction prior to the twentieth century shows an almost total neglect or denial of war as a literary topic. When it is treated in fictional works of the colonial or classic periods, it tends to be "literary" war, as in the romances of Simms or Cooper. Aside from a few chapters in John DeForest's *Miss Ravenel's Conversion*, portions of two or three other largely forgotten novels, and a scattering of sketches by Ambrose Bierce, one also looks hard for much fictional depiction of Civil War combat as well.[1] The one celebrated American novel of combat about that war, Stephen Crane's *The Red Badge of Courage*, was written, as is well known, by someone who had not been in it. In sum, to get a sense of what Americans, prior to the Great War, had written about what John Keegan has called the face of battle, one goes almost exclusively to unliterary sources—letters, journals, diaries, memoirs.

World War I changed that. For the first time, in novels by John Dos Passos, Thomas Boyd, Ernest Hemingway, William March, and others, a realistic fictional depiction of the experience of modern warfare entered American literature as a significant, and even a central topic. From this opening has flowed an important tradition, including the works of James Jones, Norman Mailer, Irwin Shaw, Joseph Heller, Kurt Vonnegut, Jr., and, most recently, Philip Caputo, Tim O'Brien, Larry Heinemann, and a host of others.

In such a tradition, *Company K* makes fair claim to a twofold importance. Given its reflection of virtually all the major themes and attitudes to be found among the first generation of works of American fiction to deal realistically, from the viewpoint of the combatant, with the experience of modern war, it may be said to be the work that as much as any other helps to define for that tradition a context. At the same time, given its complex and innovative literary experimentalism, it also may be said to offer a prophecy of a number of major American experimental war-fictions to come.

Of all the features locating *Company K* contextually in the center of the nascent American tradition of war-realism engendered by the experience of World War I, the most important is the intensity of its commitment to bearing direct witness, first and foremost, to what actually happens to ordinary men in modern, mechanized, mass combat. It may in fact stand forth as *the* work of its generation which, more than any other, takes either the experience of combat itself or its concomitant effects on those who have undergone it as a single obsessive center. Only Boyd, perhaps, in *Through the Wheat*, is so consistently direct and graphic. But his depictions are also overladen with a naturalistic stylization that often, as with Dos Passos as well in *Three Soldiers*, works at the expense of one's sensation of the experiential and actual. As with Hemingway, mixed with the violence and the brutalization, there is some talk of loss of illusion, of betrayal through patriotic lies. Yet in March, more than in any of his contemporaries, this too is ultimately subsumed into a depth of horror that goes far beyond any Lost Generation conceit. Here, individual soldiers come relentlessly forward, one after the other, the living and the dead commingled, to offer grim first-person testimony; and in narrative after narrative, there is mainly just one fundamental fact of modern warfare: the fact of violent, ugly, obscene death. Men die of gas, gunshot, grenade. They die by the bayonet. They are literally disintegrated by high explosive. They commit suicide. They murder prisoners. They murder each other. They kill wantonly and at random, at times in error and virtually always against whatever small portion they can recall of their better instincts. Killing and dying, dying and killing, they have lost touch with any fact of life save the fact of death's absolute dominion. This final reality March insists on to the degree that he often seems to have less in common with his fellow Americans than with his British poet-contemporaries such as Wilfred Owen, Robert Graves, and Siegfried Sassoon. And, as with the latter, the death depicted is never gallant sacrifice. It is not grand, valorous, brave death. It is bowel-ripping, head-shattering, body-rending death. It is the kind of death that makes men scream for their mothers, soil their trousers, dissolve themselves into whimpering wrecks. Moreover, it is death on the whole vast scale of modern mechanization.

Emblematic of this grim omnipotence is an incident, described early in the text, in which a patrol, on the word of a stupid, inexperienced, obstinate lieutenant, is ordered into a forward position where their movement will be observed and their location registered by a distinguishing clump of trees. Across the way, unseen enemy observers issue forth an instant communication. Minutes later the patrol has received a direct hit from artillery they will likewise never have seen or engaged. One body will be found wholly eviscerated, split from belly to chin, its vitals exploded in an instant by metal death from miles away. When the other dead are found, they are all without faces (62). The single survivor, spared apparently for no reason in particular, stands silent and erect, "looking down at his hand, from which the fingers had been shot away" (62).

The other feature of *Company K* contextualizing so much of American war fiction is the degree to which its thematic center—random, mindless, mass-production death—finds its precise formal correlative in a single dominant mode: irony. Sometimes particular ironies are gross and overt, such as in the chapter entitled "The Unknown Soldier." A mortally wounded young American hangs entangled in the barbed wire of No Man's Land and plays out the rage of his dying. He rails against the monument-makers and speech-givers. *His* name at least, he assures himself, will not be thus profaned. With a dying gesture, he flings away his identification tags, insuring his anonymity. What he cannot know, of course, is that it is exactly this anonymity that will lead to his dead body's enshrinement as the ultimate icon of patriotism (178–181). Or, in a scene highly reminiscent of Snowden's death in Joseph Heller's *Catch-22*, Private Wilbur Bowden carefully bandages what he believes to be a relatively minor leg wound sustained by a comrade and then, banteringly, urges the latter to rest until a rescue party arrives. Bowden recalls that the wounded soldier, even as he speaks, has seemed to have fallen into a peaceful sleep. Eventually, the rescuers come. The soldier has been found, but it turns out that he has died a good deal earlier of an enormous wound in his side that has gone wholly unnoticed (159–161). His legs are completely intact.

xvi

INTRODUCTION

Most of the ironies, however, in *Company K* are not nearly so spectacular. Rather, the atmosphere is one of something like ironic matter-of-factness. To use the telling phrase applied by Paul Fussell—himself echoing that master ironist of the matter-of-fact, Thomas Hardy—to describe the British experience of the trenches, the war is likewise in the main for the Americans of *Company K* largely "a satire of circumstance." Indeed, much of the horror of the book lies in the fact that horror itself ultimately comes to seem so everyday. Narrative after narrative unfolds, the one at hand often compounding or elaborating on matters contained in one or a number of others. For the most part, they are simple, sober, queerly unemotional. One after another, average men talk about terrible things that generally seem to have happened mainly just because they have happened. After taking a machine-gun nest, Private Carroll Hart empties his pistol into a badly wounded German who has tried to reach inside his coat. Hart opens the man's palm and finds no grenade, no pistol, but only the photograph of a little girl (65). A group of Private Philip Wadsworth's comrades conspire with a French prostitute to help the demure Wadsworth lose his virginity. He contracts a venereal disease, and is court-martialed and sent to a labor battalion (105–107). Private Leo Brogan tells of how a young French girl's pet fawn mysteriously cleaves to the company chowhound, Private Hymie White. In a touching scene, the child refuses to sell the fawn to White, but subsequently gives it to him as a present. Later that night the soldier cuts its throat with a breadknife. He has wanted it all along for stew (185–194).

So throughout *Company K*, the narratives of individual soldiers become a litany of callousness, brutality, and degradation. This is most clearly reflected in a single incident lodged both literally and figuratively at the center of the book, something that might be thought of as the novel's primal scene: the execution of twenty-two German prisoners. The order, as a series of narratives tell us, is passed down from Captain to Sergeant to the Corporal who leads the detail. Otherwise good and decent men recoil, yet now participate in mass murder. Private Walter Drury, the one soldier who refuses the order and runs is subsequently sentenced to twenty years in prison (128–129). His friend, Private Charles Gordon, remains, and, as he fires, sees the enormity of the deed in all the fullness of its awful truth. " 'Everything I was ever taught to believe about mercy, justice and virtue is a lie,' " he thinks. " 'But the biggest lie of all are the words, "God is Love." That is really the most terrible lie that man ever thought of ' " (130–132). Meanwhile, the thing done, Private Roger Inabinett rummages nonchalantly among the bodies for valuables and souvenirs (133–134). On Sunday, we are told by Private Howard Nettleton, they are all ordered to go to church (138–139).

At war's end, the survivors go home, nearly all, save those too stupid or callous to know better, carrying with them their private horrors and, in many cases, moving ahead as well into new ones. Private Everett Qualls, who has participated in the massacre, sees a blight on his farm and his family as retribution and dies a suicide (221–223). Private William Nugent, telling of the same incident and spewing his hatred of "cops" and "preachers" dies in the electric chair for murdering a policeman (209–211). Private Ralph Nerion, edging ever toward terminal madness, writhes in old army memories of petty persecutions and in new paranoiac dreams of sedition (212–213). Private Arthur Crenshaw comes home a hero who can't get a loan for a chicken farm from the banker who, the day before, has served as toastmaster at a banquet in Crenshaw's honor (219–220). Private Walter Webster returns to his intended only to find that he is too maimed to marry (226–227). Private Leslie Jourdan sits in Birmingham running a paint factory, a once-brilliant pianist with a wrecked hand (230–231). Artillery still in his head, Private Howard Virtue protests his sanity—the very cousin of Christ, he proclaims himself—sitting alone in a madhouse (241–242). Private Manuel Burt is driven to insanity by dream visitations of a young German soldier whom he has bayoneted in the roof of the mouth (245–253).[2] In the incident itself, he has been unable to remove the knife that he has driven into his enemy's brain. Now, in the aftermath, neither is he able to remove the knife of memory lodged in his own.

Meanwhile, the world goes on. Private Colin Wiltsee tells a Sunday-school story about battlefield conversion and beautiful death and ends with a paean to "the Creator of the Universe and President Hoover" and the injunction "that we must always obey their will without asking questions! . . ." (225). A warmongering ex-officer, Lieutenant James Fairbrother, inveighs against "pacifist propagandists" and heaps venom on Japan, England, Germany, France. He is running for Congress (255–256).

So ends *Company K* on a note of literal prophecy, and one that links it with other prescient works such as Dos Passos's *1919* or Hemingway's *in our time*. At home, it is soon political business as usual. Abroad, the armies quickly again begin to march.

In contrast, for the literary prophecy of *Company K* to be realized, it would take yet another highly experimental novel of yet another great war to come. That novel would be Joseph Heller's *Catch-22*. Furthermore, it would not be insignificant that *Catch-22* itself would wait to be produced and find fame not in World War II's immediate aftermath or in the complacent and prosperous decade of the fifties that followed but rather in the turbulent sixties. For *Catch-22*, as Alfred Kazin has so eloquently put it, if "ostensibly about the 1941–45 war," is also "really about The Next War, and thus about a war that will be without limits and without meaning, a war that will end only when no one is alive to fight it" (*Bright Book of Life*, 83). And, in retrospective light of the particular Next War about to be fought, the bitter, unpopular, endlessly destructive one committing to the flames a new lost generation—as well as everything in its path—in the jungles of Vietnam, this may well be the main reason why *Catch-22* in particular seems to image itself forth in so significant a number of ways as *Company K*'s thematic and formal correlative.[3] For despite all the magnitude and slaughter, World War II would remain for most Americans, in terms both moral and political, an essentially acceptable war, even, as Studs Terkel has put it, "The Good War." Accordingly, in most of the "big" novels of the war—*The Naked and the Dead* and *From Here to Eternity*, and later, *Catch-22* and *Slaughterhouse-Five*, would be notable exceptions—while the individual combatant in most cases might undergo the most violent and graphic forms of disillusionment and brutalization, there would still be about the war itself a sense of overall justification subsuming particular ironies and brutalities into larger notions of individual and collective necessity. It would take Vietnam to bring most fully into relief once again the old ironies, the betrayal of young men by speech-makers and policy-mouthers, brass hats, bureaucrats, ideologues, and political time-servers. And it took Heller's book, standing on the boundary between World War II and Vietnam, to remind Americans that the old ironies had probably not gone away at all, but had simply been assimilated into a war-breeding system so all-sufficient and monolithic as to absorb and subsume virtually any form of human objection. The result, as with March, is a totalizing irony, and with concomitant thematic and formal results.

The basic textual resemblances alone between *Company K* and *Catch-22* are often in themselves startling and suggestive. Although not narrated in the first-person used by March, virtually all the chapters in *Catch-22*, for instance, bear the names of individual combatants. As the book unfolds, we find that a good number of them are already dead, their names and their experiences totally absorbed into the dismal roll-call of sacrifices to a whole vast, impassive, war-breeding system. This fictive-temporal arrangement also enables, as with *Company K*, a narrative structure capable of moving backward and forward in the order of events and actions, with incidents, scenes, episodes, images, often prefigured far before the moment of their particular depiction and often later reduplicated in multiple, prismatic after-image. In both novels, such strategies of recurrent imaging culminate themselves in a focusing of symbolic energies on a single primal scene—in *Company K* the execution of the prisoners and in *Catch-22* the death of Snowden—that becomes a master-image of the war-world at large. In sum, a novel formed again, as with *Company K*, from a collocation of individual fragments, becomes a vast, enormous testament to the utter insignificance of individuality in a world of modern, mass-production war.[4]

As may have been suggested, the dominant irony representative of *Company K* becomes, in *Catch-22*, global and all-consuming. March's literal, rather straight-faced "satire of circumstance" takes a final step in evolution into wholesale manic absurdity. War becomes a slapstick phantasmagoria of random annihilation, at once somehow giddy and terrifying in equal measure. There is no room here even for ironic indignation, but only sublime ironic indifference. Joke mixes with atrocity, pratfall with hideous incident and accident, often commingled and, horrifically, even conflated. A bungler-God who, in the words of the protagonist Yossarian, probably couldn't get a job "as even a shipping clerk" (178), presides over a vast black comedy of death ultimately absorbing all of creation into its teeming maw. Yet, as with the madness that comes to pervade *Company K*, the nonstop hysterics of *Catch-22* should not blind us to the true center that unites it with its predecessor. It is all there, Yossarian sees, in the secret he reads in Snowden's spilled guts: "Man was matter, that was Snowden's secret. Drop him out a window and he'll fall. Set fire to him and he'll burn. Bury him and he'll rot like other kinds of garbage. The spirit gone, man is garbage. That was Snowden's secret. Ripeness was all" (429–430). It is but a post-modern variation on March's Private Charles Gordon. "God is Love." "Ripeness is all." The big lines in literature are empty self-parodic lies. The "literary" irony of *Catch-22*, as with *Company K*, points us relentlessly back toward its obsessive thematic center. As Alfred Kazin has again perceptively written, "the impressive emotion in *Catch-22* is not 'black humor,' the 'totally absurd,' those current articles of liberal politics, but horror" (p. 84).[5]

As might have been predicted, it would also be in the literature of the Vietnam war itself, however, that the prophetic dimension of March's work would find further creative realization; and it would do so, not surprisingly, in

INTRODUCTION

works that would represent the further issuing-forth of American war narrative into new forms hitherto unseen in its precincts. One would be the oral history. As in *Company K*, in works such as Al Santoli's *Everything We Had* and Wallace Terry's *Bloods*, the tale of war would be told by individual participants in their own voices, the composite effect of their narratives leading us toward larger patterns of insight and meaning.[6] Another work, Mark Baker's *Nam* would go further, to put under various topical headings composite narratives of multiple anonymous voices speaking from a wide collocation of perspectives, all adding up to something like a master narrative of the war at large. John Clark Pratt's *Vietnam Voices* would in turn take *this* one step further to dissolve the very boundaries between fact and fiction, life and art, memory and imagining. The result would be a five-act narrative tragedy comprised of materials gathered from everything from journal, diary, memoir, novel, poem, play, to mission order, policy document, news report, popular song, G.I. anecdote, advertising slogan, and latrine graffito. The effect of this highly original work can perhaps best be described as something like mass-media assault. It is the whole dreadful blare and babble of noise, pain, confusion, and waste that was the war. Yet, not surprisingly, the germ of that idea turns out to have been spoken, almost to a word, nearly half a century earlier, and spoken, in fact, by the very first voice we hear in William March's *Company K*. Contemplating the book he has completed about the war—presumably the one we are reading—Private Joseph Delaney thinks, " 'I wish there were some way to take these stories and pin them to a large wheel, each story hung on a different peg until the circle was completed. Then I would like to spin the wheel, faster and faster, until the things of which I have written took

life and were recreated, and became part of the wheel, flowing toward each other, and into each other, blurring and
then blending together into a composite whole, an unending
circle of pain. . . . That would be the picture of war. And
the sound that the wheel made, and the sound that the
men themselves made as they laughed, cried, cursed or
prayed, would be, against the falling of walls, the rushing of
bullets, the exploding of shells, the sound that war, itself,
makes . . .' " (13–14). Compare now, the latest evolution of
the motif as we find it in one of the most accomplished experimental works about the war in Vietnam, Michael Herr's
incomparable *Dispatches*: "Holy war, long-nose jihad like a
face-off between one god who would hold the coonskin to
the wall while we nailed it up, and another whose detach-
ment would see the blood run out of ten generations, if that
was how long it took for the wheel to go around" (45).

To cite one of the popular songs of the Vietnam era, it is
as ever, "the circle within the circle, the wheel within the
wheel." As the new literature of Vietnam continues even now
to show, Delaney was right. And thus was the prophetic
power of the artist who created him, William March.

Notes

1. It is instructive to note, for instance, that out of sixteen chapters in Edmund Wilson's *Patriotic Gore*, only two address fiction.
Similarly, it is notable that none of the three greatest postwar real-
ists, Twain, Howells, and James, saw significant military action.
Similarly, aside from Twain's account, in "The Private History of a
Campaign that Failed," of his brief foray with border-state militia
and from small echoes of the war in Howells and James, all three
seemed to show an almost perverse lack of interest in the conflict—

surely the most crucial experience of their American generation—as a subject of literary depiction.

2. As suggested by the bayoneting incident described in my earlier remarks on March's own experience in the war, this episode must surely be autobiographical in origin—although now powerfully transformed with the wound, in a novel full of "voices" trying to speak the horror of the war, to the brain by way of the roof of the dead man's mouth. So also one must consider the similarly powerful transmutation of autobiographical reference in an earlier narrative where Private Leslie Westmore suffers an episode of hysterical blindness. See Simmonds, 23 and 190–92.

3. I have already remarked on the strong affinities of *Company K* with the works of British soldier-memoirists and soldier-poets such as Owen, Graves, and Sassoon. In this regard, it strikes me as significant that Paul Fussell, in *The Great War and Modern Memory*, also draws recurrent connections between *Catch-22* and the literature of the British experience of the trenches.

4. In neither case should this be judged an argument for some totalizing "structure." As Roy S. Simmonds records, March never really could settle on organization, and published a number of "Company K" narratives separately and, in some cases, in various versions. See *The Two Worlds of William March*, 45, 49, and 60. As to Heller, it is also difficult in the same vein to dispute Norman Mailer's observation that one could extract one hundred pages from "anywhere in the middle of *Catch-22*, and not even the author could be certain they were gone."

5. To the degree that this new vision of "horror" in the American literature of war arises out of the relentless depiction of war itself as a network of paranoiac congruencies, my discussion of the prophetic dimension of *Company K* might also be extended, I believe, toward other major works such as *Slaughterhouse Five* and *Gravity's Rainbow*.

6. In the Vietnam novel, the form has also been most recently recapitulated in Larry Heinemann's *Paco's Story*, winner of the 1987 National Book Award. There, as in *Company K*, dead men

once again do tell tales of war, of the memory of war, and of the war-haunted lives of its broken survivors.

Works Cited

Fussell, Paul. *The Great War and Modern Memory*. New York: Oxford University Press, 1975.

Heller, Joseph. *Catch-22*. New York: Simon and Schuster, 1961.

Herr, Michael. *Dispatches*. New York: Alfred A. Knopf, 1977.

Kazin, Alfred. *Bright Book of Life*. Boston: Little, Brown, 1973.

Keegan, John. *The Face of Battle*. New York: Viking Press, 1976.

March, William. *Company K*. New York: Harrison Smith and Robert Haas, 1933.

Simmonds, Roy S. *The Two Worlds of William March*. University, Ala.: University of Alabama Press, 1983.

Terkel, Studs. *The Good War*. New York: Pantheon, 1984.

COMPANY
K

ROSTER

PRIVATE JOSEPH DELANEY

WE have had supper and my wife and I are sitting on our porch. It will not be dark for an hour yet and my wife has brought out some sewing. It is pink and full of lace and it is something she is making for a friend of hers who is going to be married soon.

All about us are our neighbors, sprinkling their lawns, or sitting on their porches, as we are doing. Occasionally my wife and I speak to some friend who passes, and bows, or stops to chat for a moment, but mostly we sit silent. . . .

I am still thinking of the book which I have just completed. I say to myself: "I have finished my book at last, but I wonder if I have done what I set out to do?"

Then I think: "This book started out to be a record of my own company, but I do not want it to be that, now. I want it to be a record of every company in every army. If its cast and its overtones are American, that is only because the American scene is the one that I know. With different names and different settings, the men of whom I have written could, as easily, be French, German, English or Russian for that matter."

I think: "I wish there were some way to take these

stories and pin them to a huge wheel, each story hung
on a different peg until the circle was completed. Then
I would like to spin the wheel, faster and faster, until
the things of which I have written took life and were
recreated, and became part of the wheel, flowing toward
each other, and into each other; blurring, and then
blending together into a composite whole, an unending circle of pain. . . . That would be the picture of
war. And the sound that the wheel made, and the sound
that the men themselves made as they laughed, cried,
cursed or prayed, would be, against the falling of walls,
the rushing of bullets, the exploding of shells, the sound
that war, itself, makes. . . ."

We had been silent for a long time, and then my
wife spoke: "I'd take out the part about shooting
prisoners."

"Why?" I asked.

"Because it is cruel and unjust to shoot defenseless
men in cold blood. It may have been done a few times,
I'm not denying that, but it isn't typical. It couldn't
have happened often."

"Would a description of an air raid be better?" I
asked. "Would that be more humane? Would that be
more typical?"

"Yes," she said. "Yes. That happened many times, I
understand."

"Is it crueler, then, for Captain Matlock to order

prisoners shot, because he was merely stupid, and thought the circumstances warranted that, than for an aviator to bomb a town and kill harmless people who are not even fighting him?"

"That isn't as revolting as shooting prisoners," said my wife stubbornly. Then she added: "You see the aviator cannot see where his bomb strikes, or what it does, so he is not really responsible. But the men in your story had the prisoners actually before them. . . . It's not the same thing, at all."

I began to laugh with bitterness: "Possibly you are right," I said. "Possibly you have put into words something inescapable and true."

Then my wife reached out and took my hand. "You think I'm hard and unsympathetic," she said; "but I'm not, really, darling."

I sat silent after that, watching the Ellis children across the street shouting and laughing and playing on their lawn. It was early June and there was a faint breeze carrying with it the smell of spiced pinks and Cape jasmine. Gradually it got darker and my wife put away her sewing, yawned and rubbed her eyes. All about us were the green, well-kept lawns of our neighbors, with flowers in bloom and shrubs banked against walls and fences. The sight of this green, flowing smoothness made me think, somehow, of old battlefields which I have seen. . . .

You can always tell an old battlefield where many men have lost their lives. The next Spring the grass comes up greener and more luxuriant than on the surrounding countryside; the poppies are redder, the corn-flowers more blue. They grow over the field and down the sides of the shell holes and lean, almost touching, across the abandoned trenches in a mass of color that ripples all day in the direction that the wind blows. They take the pits and scars out of the torn land and make it a sweet, sloping surface again. Take a wood, now, or a ravine: In a year's time you could never guess the things which had taken place there.

I repeated my thoughts to my wife, but she said it was not difficult to understand about battlefields: The blood of the men killed on the field, and the bodies buried there, fertilize the ground and stimulate the growth of vegetation. That was all quite natural she said.

But I could not agree with this, too-simple, explanation: To me it has always seemed that God is so sickened with men, and their unending cruelty to each other, that he covers the places where they have been as quickly as possible.

PRIVATE ROWLAND GEERS

IT had snowed steadily, and the Virginia countryside was white and still; close-order drill was impossible that day, so Captain Matlock took us for a long hike across the hills. Coming back, our spirits were so high that we began to double time of our own accord, shouting at the tops of our voices and hitting each other with snowballs. We came to the top of the hill and looked down. It was almost dusk, and below us, in the valley, lights began to show in the barracks. Then Ted Irvine gave a shout and ran down the hill, and in a moment we had all broken ranks, rushing after him, pushing and laughing and piling into the bunk houses.

It was an hour before supper, so Walt Webster and I decided to have a bath, but when we got to the bath house, we found there was no hot water there, and for a minute we stood with our clothes off, shivering. Then, we held our breath and ran under the cold shower, jumping up and down and hitting each other on the chest, until a warm glow began to flow through our bodies. "This is great," I said. "This is great, Walt!"

But Walt who was singing senselessly, at the top of his lungs, merely because he was young and full of life, stopped suddenly, and picked me up in his powerful arms, carrying me to the bath house door, trying to throw me into a snow bank. But I locked my legs around him and held on, and we both went into the bank together. We floundered about in the snow wrestling and laughing. The other boys in the bunk house saw us and soon every man in the company was naked and wallowing in the snow, shouting with exhilaration.

Walt stood up, slapped his thighs, and began to crow like a cock. "Bring on the whole German army!" he shouted. "Bring them on all together, or one at a time. I can whip them all!"

CORPORAL JERRY BLANDFORD

SITTING next to me at the counter was a sweet-look-
ing girl, or rather she was a grown woman, twenty-
eight or thirty years old, and we got to talking. I
reached over and took her check, but she put up a kick.
"I think I ought to be the one to be paying the check,"
she said laughingly. Then we went out of the drug
store and walked down the street. I told her how I had
looked forward to my leave and how disappointed I was.
It wasn't much fun when you didn't know anybody. I
didn't have any place to go in particular, so I was walking in her direction, but finally she said she had to turn.
"Well, good-by," she said, and held out her hand.

"Don't leave me," I said. "Come on to the hotel and
stay with me. I'm not insulting you," I said. "I respect
you. I'm not trying to insult you."

She thought a minute and then shook her head.

"I just want you to be with me," I said. "I want to
smell cologne on a woman and I want to see her with
her hair down. I won't do anything that you don't want
me to do. I won't even touch you, unless you say it's
all right. . . ."

"You must have a very poor opinion of me, to think

I'm the sort of woman you can pick up on the street."

"No," I said, "I respect you. If I didn't respect you, I wouldn't ask you to come. If I wanted a street-walker, I could get fifty, and you know it. I respect you," I said; "I really do."

She stood there, looking at me. Then she shook her head. "I'm sorry," she said.

"I'm going across next week," I said. "I may be killed in a month. I may never have a chance to be with a decent woman again. . . ."

Then suddenly she made up her mind. "Very well," she said, "I'll come. I'll stay with you every minute of the time until your leave is up. Go get your things and we'll go to another hotel and register as man and wife."

"I'll be careful not to embarrass you. I won't make any breaks, or let any of the boys know."

"I don't care," she said. "I don't care who knows. I wouldn't come at all if I cared about that." Then she slipped her arm through mine and we walked away.

CORPORAL PIERRE BROCKETT

WE knew they wouldn't sell to soldiers in uniform as a rule, but this bar was out of the way, and we figured we might talk the bartender into it. So all three of us went in and lined up.

"Well, what will you gentlemen have?" asked the bartender in a polite voice.

"Give me a rye straight," I said.

"Give me rye with a beer chaser," said Bill Anderson.

"I'll take Scotch," said Barney Fathers.

The bartender picked up a bottle and then put it down again. "Are you boys in a big hurry?" he asked.

"No," we all said together, "oh, no, we got lots of time!"

"All right, then," said the bartender; "just stand there until war is over and I'll be glad to shake up them drinks."

PRIVATE ARCHIE LEMON

THE fourth day out was a Sunday, and that morning the Captain held services on deck. It was December, but the sun was shining on the surrounding water, its light reflected blindingly in the ship's brass. It was almost too warm, in the sunlight, for the heavy overcoats we wore. We stood there for a while, and then the services began. They were very simple: a hymn, a prayer and a short sermon. Then, at the end, a benediction in which the chaplain asked God to give our hearts courage, and our arms strength, to strike down our adversaries. He said we were not soldiers, in the accepted sense of the word: We were crusaders who had dedicated our lives and our souls to our country and to our God that the things we revere and hold sacred, might not perish.

When we got back to our quarters, we were all silent and thoughtful. We lay on our bunks thinking of the chaplain's words. Sylvester Keith, whose bunk was next to mine, gave me a cigarette, and lit one himself. "The chaplain has got the right dope," he said: "I mean about saving civilization and dedicating our lives to our country."

Bob Nalls had come up, and joined us. "I've been thinking over what he said about this being the war to end injustice. I don't mind getting killed to do a thing of that sort. I don't mind, since the people coming after me will live in happiness and peace. . . ."

Then we sat there smoking our cigarettes and thinking.

CORPORAL WALTER ROSE

GOING across in the transport, I was picked for a special submarine guard. Each man in our detail was given a pair of glasses and assigned a certain angle of water to watch, so that the entire horizon was constantly observed. My angle was 247 to 260 and in the tower with me was Les Yawfitz, whose angle joined mine. There was a telephone by each of us which communicated with the engine room below and the gun crews standing by on deck.

Late one afternoon, when it was cold and raining, I saw a tomato crate floating on the water. I looked at it for a long time, trying to make up my mind if it was moving with the tide. Then when I'd about decided that it was, I noticed it had moved backward a foot or two, contrary to the direction of the waves. I grabbed my 'phone and reported to the gunners, and the engineers, that there was a periscope concealed under the crate. The transport swung to one side quickly, and at the same moment the gunners began to fire. Immediately we saw a submarine come to the top, flounder, and turn sidewise in a burst of steam.

Everybody gave me the old glad-hand and wanted to

know how I could tell that the tomato crate camouflaged a periscope. I didn't know, as a matter of fact, I just guessed right; that's all: So I was an intelligent hero, and got the Navy Cross. If I'd been wrong, and there'd been nothing under the crate, I would have been a dumb bastard, a disgrace to the outfit, and, like as not, would have been thrown into the brig. They're not fooling me any.

PRIVATE SAMUEL UPDIKE

IT felt good to be on solid land again after fourteen days on a crowded transport. Our hobnailed boots clattered on the cobblestones, as we marched at ease down the main street of the town and up the hill that led to the barracks. It was cold, but the sun was out, and everybody was in high spirits, and full of fun. We laughed and shoved each other about. Then Rowland Geers passed his pack and rifle to Fred Willcoxen and began to turn handsprings, and clown. But the French people stood there looking at us, with their mouths open, a surprised expression on their faces. They weren't at all like an American crowd: We tried to joke and kid them, but they wouldn't answer. They just looked at us like we were crazy, and turned their heads away.

"What's the matter with these people?" asked Tom Stahl. "Where's their pep? Where's their spirit?"

"Everybody is wearing black," I said. "You'd think they'd just come from a funeral."

Then a woman in the crowd, standing near the curb, answered me in a broad, English voice: "The people wearing black are in mourning," she said, as if she were speaking to a child. "We're having a war, you know."

"Oh, I didn't realize!" I said. "I'm sorry, I really am!" But the English woman had turned and walked away.

I've thought many times afterwards what clowns we must have seemed.

SERGEANT MICHAEL RIGGIN

ONE thing that puzzles me about these new men is why they are always writing letters home, or getting packages from their mothers or sweethearts. You didn't see much of that in the old days, when I came into the service. Most of the boys then didn't have any people to write to, and the only letters they got were from strumpets they'd met while on liberty. But, as I said, these new men are always writing letters and sending letters off. I can't understand that.

I was raised in an orphan asylum, myself. No chance of anybody who was raised in an orphan asylum, under Mrs. McMallow's care being homesick. . . . I'll never forget the old Tartar. She had a long, bony face and yellow teeth. She pulled her hair back as tight as she could, and pinned it to her head. She talked in a sharp, worried voice. She wasn't very good to any of the kids, but she used to pick on me more than the others.— Well, I guess I gave her more trouble than the others. She said she'd break my stubbornness, and I guess she'd a-done it, too, if I hadn't run away when I was fourteen, because I couldn't stand it any longer.

I don't mean she beat me. She never done that. (Unless I damned well deserved it, of course, and then it didn't hurt much.) She was just mean. . . . This'll give you an idea: When I was nine years old, I cut my foot on a piece of glass and the doctor had to sew it up. That night Mrs. McMallow came to the hospital to see how I was getting along. (Oh, she always done what she thought was her duty, all right.) She had made a bowl of soup with macaroni in it, knowing that I liked macaroni soup better than anything else. When I realized she had made the soup just for me, I put my arms out and pulled her down on the bed beside me. I wanted her to take me in her arms, and kiss me, but I didn't know how to ask her to do it, so I reached up and tried to kiss her, but she pulled her face away quickly and took my hands off her arm. "Michael Riggin," she said, "how many times have I told you to keep your finger nails clean!" Then I picked up the bowl of macaroni soup and threw it across the room. I wouldn't have eaten a spoonful of it to save my life. . . .

That's what I mean about these fellows writing home all the time. I can't understand it. That's all a bunch of hooey. Anybody who cares for anybody else is a God damned fool, if you ask me! I don't care a hoot for anything there is: Take all you can get, I say, and don't give anything in return, if you can help it.

SERGEANT THEODORE DONOHOE

IF you worked for a grocer or a candy maker, or even an undertaker, and went around talking about what inferior groceries, or candy, your employer sold, or how unsatisfactory all funerals were, you would not, unless you were a fool, expect any advancement or honors in your chosen business or profession, would you? Then why in the name of heaven do otherwise intelligent men like Leslie Yawfitz or Walter Rose talk contemptuously about the mismanagement, waste and stupidity of war and then expect to receive promotions or decorations, becoming sullen and dissatisfied when those things fail to appear?

I tell you war is a business, like anything else, and if you get anywhere in it, you've got to adjust yourself to its peculiarities and play your cards the way they fall.

CAPTAIN TERENCE L. MATLOCK

WHEN my platoon sergeants had assembled, I I read the order granting liberty to fifty men from each company. . . . "Trucks will pick up the liberty party at two o'clock, this afternoon, at Regimental Headquarters, and the same trucks will be waiting for the men in Celles-le-Cher in front of the Y.M.C.A. hut, until eight o'clock, Sunday night," I read. Then we went over the company roster, squad by squad, and picked the men who were to go. Sergeant Dunning looked at his watch. It was 11:10. "I guess the boys will have to hurry to make that two o'clock truck," he said. My other sergeants moved away also, but I stopped them.

"Before these men go on liberty, I want their equipment shined up; their rifles cleaned and oiled, and their extra clothes washed and hung on the line to dry." The sergeants saluted me and turned to go.

"Yes, sir," they said.

"Wait a minute," I continued. "Don't be so fast: I'll inspect the rifles and equipment of the liberty party at 12:30 in the billets. Then, at 1 P.M. have each man report to me, outside the office, with his extra clothes washed and wrung out. . . . And tell the men they'd better wash them clean! . . ."

Promptly at one o'clock the men began lining up outside the company office, their uniforms scraped and brushed, their faces shining. It had rained the night before and they picked their way across the muddy courtyard, so as not to soil their boots, which had been rubbed with a mixture of soot and dubbing. Across the arm of each man were the clothes he had washed out.

I sat at a table in the courtyard with Sergeant Boss, my top sergeant, and Corporal Waller, my clerk, who had the passes made out and ready for the men, beside me. Then the first man, Private Calhoun, came up and spread his clothes on the table. I opened them up, looking carefully at the seams.

"Is that your idea of a clean pair of drawers?" I asked.

"That's mildew," he said; "I tried, but I couldn't get it out, sir."

"Well, go back and try some more," I said.

Calhoun turned away, and as he did somebody at the rear of the line gave me the raspberry.

"Who did that?" I asked.

Nobody answered.

The second man had placed his clothes on the table. I picked them up and threw them in the mud without looking at them. Then as each man came up with his clothes, I took them from his arm and threw them into the mud-puddle. After that, I took the passes from Waller, tore them into tiny pieces and scattered them on a pile of manure. . . .

"When you men have learned to respect your commanding officer, things are going to be better all the way round," I said.

FIRST SERGEANT PATRICK BOSS

I'VE seen some pretty bad outfits in my time, but this one takes the cake. In the old days men knew how to soldier and how to take care of themselves. They were tough birds all right, but they knew discipline, and they respected the officers over them because the officers respected them, too. In the first place, you had to be an A No. 1 man to get in: They weren't taking just anything in those days.—Well, they've let the bars down now, all right! Look at the riffraff we get.—Half of them, right now, don't know the difference between the orders "right front into line" and "on right into line." Part of the company starts to execute one command, and a part another, while some of the men just stand still, looking about them helplessly. I've tried to beat it into their thick heads. I've tried and tried.—Christ, it's enough to make a man tear out his hair, I tell you! . . .

In the old days they used to say that a company with a good top sergeant didn't need a captain. I guess that's true. I don't want to throw any bouquets at myself, but if it wasn't true, I don't know what would become of *this* one. Nit-wit Terry—that ribbon-selling wonder!

FIRST SERGEANT PATRICK BOSS

. . . How do men like him get a commission, anyway? It beats me. It's over my head. Well, anyway, I'm getting out of the outfit when this hitch is done. It's not like it was in the old days, when a man could really have some self-respect.

PRIVATE ROGER JONES

I NEVER saw the trenches so quiet as they were that time at Verdun. There wasn't a squarehead in sight, and except for the fact that they fired a machine gun every once in a while, and sent up a rocket, you wouldn't have known there was anybody ahead of us at all. Everything would be very quiet when suddenly the rocket would go whizzing up and the machine gun would splutter a time or two. Then a few minutes later another rocket would go off, farther down the trench, and there would be a dozen more machine gun bullets to go with it.

The boys made up a story that there wasn't anybody in front of us except an old man, who rode a bicycle, and his wooden legged wife. The man would ride down the duckboards, with his wife running behind him carrying the machine gun. Then the man would stop and send up a rocket, while the old woman fired the gun. After that they started all over, and kept it up all night.

The boys talked about the old German, and his wife with the wooden leg, until, after a while, everybody began to believe they were actually there.

"It's just like a German to make his wife run behind him and carry the heavy gun," said Emile Ayres one night. "They all beat their wives, too, I've heard it said."

"That's a lie!" said Jakie Brauer whose mother and father were both born in Germany. "Germans are as good to their wives as Americans, or anybody else!"

"Then why don't he carry the gun sometime?" Emile asked; "why don't he carry the gun and let the old woman ride on the bicycle?"

PRIVATE CARTER ATLAS

FOR breakfast weak coffee, a thin slice of bread and a dipper full of watery soup; for dinner two soggy potatoes, with dirt still clinging to their jackets, a piece of meat the size of a man's thumb and a spoonful of jam; for supper more coffee, but weaker this time, and a pan full of unseasoned rice.—How can a man keep going on such rations? But try to get more! Try and see what happens to you!

I thought about food all the time: I remembered all the good meals I had ever eaten and thought of rare dishes, such as truffles or ortolans, which I had read about, but never tasted. I used to plan my first meal on the outside, but thinking about those things all the time made me so hungry, I was almost crazy. When I closed my eyes I could see a thick, luscious steak, broiled a deep brown, a lump of butter melting over it and becoming a part of its juices. I could see the steak, surrounded by tender, French fried potatoes, and smell its flavor as distinctly as if it were actually before me. I lay on my bunk with my eyes closed, gloating over the steak. . . . "In just a minute I'll cut into it, and begin to eat," I thought. . . .

Then the detail returned to the trenches, bringing our supper in a g.i. can. It was rice again, cold and clammy, and when Sergeant Donohoe gave me my part of it, I took it, hungry as I was, and dumped it in the mud. Then I went back to the dugout and lay on my bunk and cried like a baby. If they'd just give me a good meal every once in a while, I wouldn't mind this war so much!

PRIVATE LUCIEN JANOFF

MY trouble went back to that pair of shoes the supply sergeant issued me at St. Aignan. They were three sizes too big for me and they felt like they were made out of cast-iron. My heels kept blistering every time I took a hike. They were sore all the time. After a while they got callused, and they didn't blister any more, but when they quit blistering, they hurt worse than ever. I couldn't even bear to touch them, they hurt so.

Finally Roy Winters said he thought there was pus under the calluses and that was why my heels ached so. He said I ought to go to the dressing station and have them opened up. "Nothing doing!" I said. "Fat chance of me doing that! I know well enough what *those* babies will do to me: They'll give me chloroform, and when I wake up my feet will be cut off at the ankles. . . . 'What the hell you kicking about?' they'll say to me; 'your *heels* don't hurt you no more, do they?' . . . That's what they'll say.—You can't fool me. . . ."

Then Roy said he would split my heels himself and get the pus out, if I thought I could stand it. Told him to go ahead. Told him I'd stand it, all right. A fellow named Rufe Yeomans and a fellow named Charlie Upson held my legs, so I wouldn't jerk away. I said I wouldn't make a sound. Didn't either while Roy was cutting, but when he was scraping near the bone I hollered some. I couldn't help hollering a little, I guess.

PRIVATE THOMAS STAHL

IN Merlaut, where we were billeted, Wilbur Halsey and I were drawing water from the well when the bucket came off and fell to the bottom with a splash. "Wait a minute," said Wilbur; "I'll go inside and tell the old lady, and get another bucket from her." A few minutes later the old lady came running out tearing her hair and beating her breasts, with Wilbur walking behind her, trying to explain what had happened. When the old lady reached the well, it was all Wilbur and I could do to keep her from jumping after the bucket. She got more and more excited every minute.

Allan Methot, who speaks good French, came out of the billet and explained to the woman that it had been an accident, and that Wilbur and I were willing to pay for the bucket, but she knocked the money out of his hand and threw herself on the ground. A crowd of French people had gathered. They stared over the wall, and the old woman pointed at us and began to talk excitedly. Then the French people all made clucking noises and each, in turn, went to the edge of the well and peered over, shaking their heads and spreading their arms out.

"That must have been an extra fine bucket," said Wilbur. "The way they act, you'd think it was made out of platinum."

By the next day everybody in town had come to look down the well and listen to the old woman's story, and to sympathize with her. That afternoon when we got orders to move, there was a crowd around the well looking down, as if they expected the bucket to jump up into their arms, of its own accord, while the old lady wiped her eyes on the bottom of her petticoat.

"This is getting on my nerves," said Wilbur . . . "I'll be glad to get out of this place. Everybody here is nuts."

SERGEANT JAMES DUNNING

LIEUTENANT FAIRBROTHER had just been assigned to my platoon when he thought of a way
to find machine gun nests at night. He said four or five
men should fill their pockets with rocks and creep along
the German lines until they came to a clump of bushes
or a mound that looked suspicious. Then they were to
throw in a couple of rocks. If there was a machine gun
concealed, the throwing of the rocks would make the
gunners mad at us, and they would begin to fire, thus
exposing their position. Nobody cracked a smile while
he was speaking to the platoon, but when he had gone
out of the bunk house, we began to laugh.

"I think one of the men should carry a sky-rocket in
his right hand," said Frank Halligan. "Then, when the
machine gunners start firing, he can hold the rocket
between his thumb and forefinger until it is struck by
one of the passing bullets and ignited. Then the rocket
will soar into the air and fall behind the German lines,
where the Kaiser is pinning Iron Crosses on a regiment.
As the rocket comes down, the Kaiser bends over, and
the tip of the hot rocket catches him squarely on his
military butt. The Kaiser jerks forward and rubs the

place with his hands, thinking that somebody has kicked him, and that the men have mutinied. This frightens His Majesty, and he begins to run toward our lines. As he runs, the whole German army falls in behind him, trying to explain what had happened, but the Kaiser won't listen: He runs and runs until he reaches the Marne, which he tries to jump, falls short, and is drowned. Then the entire German army, out of politeness, jump in also, and are drowned, and the war is over and we all go back to the States."

Albert Nallett got up and closed the door. "Don't let anybody hear you talking like that, sarge," he said. "If they knew at Divisional about your fine military mind, they'd have bars on your shoulders and a Sam Browne buckled around your waist before you could say scat."

SERGEANT WILBUR TIETJEN

I WOULD take up a position in the line, my rifle
strapped to my shoulder, the barrel resting on the
bank, and look through my telescopic sights at the German trenches, a thousand or more yards away. (A sniper
must have patience; that is as important as ability to
shoot good.) And so I would lie there for hours, studying
the German line, which looked deserted. "There are
men there, all right," I'd say to myself, "and one of them
will get careless and show himself before long." Sure
enough, sooner or later, a head would appear over the
side of the trench or a man would crawl outside for a
minute.

Then I would figure windage and elevation, line up
my sights, slack my body, take a half-breath and squeeze
the trigger very slow. More often than not the man I
was aiming at would jump up and spin around a couple
of times before falling. He looked very comical from
where I was—like a toy soldier which somebody had
whittled being upset by the wind.

I was the best rifleman in the regiment, so everybody
said. One time, in July, I hit nine men out of a possible
twelve. The colonel was in the line that afternoon and

he and his adjutant were watching my shots with their strong field glasses. They made a lot over me when I plugged the ninth man and I grinned like a great fellow. You see, the men were so far away, it didn't seem like killing anybody, really. In fact I never thought of them as men, but as dolls, and it was hard to believe that anything as small as that could feel pain or sorrow. If there was a race of people no bigger, say, than your thumb, even the best hearted person in the world could step on one of them and not feel bad about it. When that thought came into my head, I told it to Allan Methot, but he said a fellow had already used it in a book. "Well, it's the truth, even if a book *has* been wrote about it," I said.

PRIVATE JESSE BOGAN

WE came to a long hill shaped like a semi-circle and dug in against the protected side. Below us the Germans were shelling Marigny, a small town. We could see people running out of the houses, making funny gestures, and down the narrow streets, until they joined the line that filled the highway. Then we dug in on the off side of the hill and waited.

It was late May and the whole countryside was green and beautiful. Below us, in the valley, fruit trees were in bloom, pink, white and red, running across the valley in strips of color, and spotting the side of the hill. Then a haze settled over the valley, and gradually it got dark.

The Germans had quit shelling the town. It lay demolished below us. Lieutenant Bartelstone came up: "All right, men! Get your things together. We're going in the wood when it gets dark." Then he spoke to Sergeant Dunning: "The orders are to stop the Germans and not let them advance an inch farther. . . ."

"Well, anyway," said Alex Marro, after the lieutenant had gone, "that's simple and to the point."

"What's the name of this place?" asked Art Crenshaw.

"I don't know," said Sergeant Dunning.—"What difference does that make?"

"I asked a Frenchman on the road," said Allan Methot, "and he said it was called Belleau Wood."

"Come on! Come on!" said Sergeant Dunning. "Get your equipment together, and quit chewing the fat!"

PRIVATE PHILIP CALHOUN

AL DE CASTRO and I sat crouched in a small shell hole, excited, watching the German artillerymen destroy Marigny. A shell-shocked dog was huddled against the community wash house. His tail curved under him, and the hair on his back was stiff and erect. Water ran from his eyes and his mouth slavered. Occasionally he would spin rapidly in a circle, and attempt to bite his tail; then he would stop, exhausted, and snap weakly to right and left; or occasionally he thrust his muzzle to the sky, and his jaws opened widely, but the sound of his voice was lost in the sound of the shelling.

At last little remained standing in the town except one wall of white limestone. On this wall was a religious print, in a gilt frame, showing a crown of thorns and a bleeding heart from which flames ascended; while beside it, on a wooden peg, hung a peasant's shapeless coat. I lay on my belly and stared at the wall. . . . The shells fell faster and the frightened dog began again to spin and chase his tail. The white wall trembled and a few stones fell, and when I looked up again, the coat had slipped from its peg and lay in the dust like a sprawling, dead bat. . . . Then, suddenly, the shelling stopped, and the silence that followed was terrible. The dog sniffed the air. He lifted his voice and howled.

I got up, then, and put on my pack and a moment later Al stood beside me. For a moment we both looked at the white wall, still standing, and at the sacred picture untouched in its place.

Al walked over to the wall and stood regarding it curiously: "Why should that one wall remain?" he asked. "Why should it alone be spared? . . ."

Then as he stood there adjusting his pack, and fumbling with the rusty catch of his cartridge belt, there came a tearing sound, and a sharp report; and down fell the wall in a cloud of dust, smothering the heart from which flames were ascending, and crushing him to death with its weight.

PRIVATE EDWARD ROMANO

I WAS out on observation post near Hill 44 and it was raining. There was no wind and the rain fell straight down. To the north there were flashes, like heat lightning, along the horizon, and the low growling of distant batteries. As I crouched in the trench, wet to the skin and shivering with cold, I thought: "It's quiet here to-night, but up to the north terrible things are happening: There, at this instant, men are being torn to pieces, or stabbed to death with bayonets."

A Very light went up suddenly, to break in the sky with a faint kiss, and against its flare I saw the intricate intrenchments of rusting barbed wire. I saw, too, the slow rain, gleaming like a crystal against the light, and falling in dead, unslanted lines to the field. I lay huddled and trembling in the shallow trench, my rifle pressed against my body. . . . The rain was washing up bodies of men buried hastily; there was an odor of decay in the air. . . .

I saw a man walking toward me, upright and unafraid. His feet were bare and his beautiful hair was long. I raised my rifle to kill him, but when I saw it was Christ, I lowered it again. "Would you have hurt me?"

he asked sadly. I said yes, and began to curse: "You ought to be ashamed of yourself to let this go on!— You ought to be ashamed! . . ."

But he lifted his arms to the sodden field, to the tangled wire, to the charred trees like teeth in a fleshless jaw. "Tell me what to do," he said. "Tell me what to do, if you know! . . ." It was then that I began to cry, and Christ cried, too, our tears flowing with the slow rain.

At twelve o'clock my relief came. It was Ollie Teclaw, and I wanted to tell him what I had seen, but I knew that he would only laugh at me.

LIEUTENANT EDWARD BARTELSTONE

I CAME off watch cold and sick—shivering; wet to my miserable skin. I could feel vermin itching my back and crawling over my chest. I had not bathed for weeks and my feet had blistered offensively. There was a sour, overpowering smell in the dugout, and it turned my stomach and made me want to vomit. . . . I lighted my candle and looked for a long time at my dirty hands, and my finger nails, caked with muck. A feeling of revulsion came over me. "I'll stand anything else," I said, "but I won't stand this filth any longer. . . ." I cocked my pistol and placed it on the shelf beside the candle. . . . "When it's exactly midnight, I'm going to kill myself. . . ."

On my bed were some magazines which Archie Smith had read and passed on to me. I picked one up at random, and opened it; and there looking at me with sad, pitying eyes was Lillian Gish. Never in my life have I seen anything so pure or so clean as her face. I kept wrinkling my eyes, as if unable to believe what I saw. Then I touched her cheeks with my finger, but very gently. . . . "Why, you're clean and lovely," I said in surprise. . . . "You're pure and lovely and sweet! . . ."

LIEUTENANT EDWARD BARTELSTONE

I cut out the picture and made a leather case for it, and I carried it with me as long as war lasted. I used to look at it every night before I went to bed, and every morning when I awoke. It took me safely through those terrible months and it brought me out, in the end, calm and undisturbed.

PRIVATE JACOB GELLER

ONE day a fellow named Harry Waddell and myself came upon a dead German who had fallen across a log and rested on his shoulders. He still had his light knapsack strapped to his back. (The knapsack was made of cowhide with some of the hair still on it. The hair was dark brown, with white markings, and I remember saying to Harry, at the time, it must have come off a Holstein.)

When Harry and I looked at the man good we saw that he had been killed by a piece of h.e. There was a hole in his chest as big as your fist. Harry and I went through him for souvenirs, but he didn't have anything except a few photographs of his family, and some letters, which we put back in his pocket, in accordance with regulations. Then we turned him over on his belly to see what he had in his knapsack. There was blood all over the knapsack, too, and there was nothing in it except a pair of winter drawers, and a half loaf of brown German bread.

"That's luck," said Harry, "we can eat the bread!"

My mouth commenced to water and I could feel my stomach growling, but when we looked at the bread close we saw that it was covered with blood. (The bread was what the Heinies called pumpernickel, and it was still a little soggy on the inside where the blood hadn't dried out.)

I took out my knife and tried to scrape off the blood, but when I saw that it went all the way through, I gave up that idea.

"Don't waste the bread that way!" said Harry. So I cut it in two equal parts and Harry Waddell and me ate every crumb of it.

PRIVATE WALTER LANDT

IT was only a small flesh wound, but Lieutenant Bartelstone thought I'd better go back to the dressing station and take a shot of anti-tetanus anyway. When I got there, the two doctors couldn't decide which was the best way to give it to me. The tall doctor thought it should be injected directly into the stomach, and so I pulled up my shirt while he jabbed me, but the glass tube broke, and most of the fluid spilled down my leg. Then the fat doctor said his partner was doing it all wrong, and I took down my pants while he jabbed me in the stern. But his tube broke, too, and then it was the tall doctor's turn to laugh and make humorous remarks. They kept me there, pulling up my shirt, and taking down my pants, for about an hour, while each argued the merits of his method, and tried to get a full shot into me without breaking the tube. The fourth time the tall doctor punctured my belly, my arms and legs were beginning to swell. Then I remember the other doctor saying: "All right, soldier, take down your pants again and we'll show him how it really ought to be done!" After that everything got black, and the room started whirling.

That's all I remember, but they tell me I hollered without stopping, for two days and two nights, and that I swelled up bigger than a dead nigger who has been lying in a shell hole for a week. Next time I get wounded, I'll have lockjaw and enjoy it.

PRIVATE GRALEY BORDEN

W E were detached temporarily from our division and assigned to the French, and for six days and nights we were fighting without sleep and without rest. Since we were fighting under French orders, we drew supplies and food with them also. When the first food arrived, there was red wine and a small ration of cognac for each of us. We were hungry, cold, and very tired, and the cognac warmed our blood, and made the long nights bearable.

But on the second day, when rations were delivered again, the wine and the cognac were missing from the allowance of the American soldiers. The religious organizations in France had protested against rationing intoxicants to us: It was feared the news would get back to the United States, and that the Woman's Christian Temperance Union and the Methodist Board of Temperance and Public Morals would hear of it and would not be pleased.

LIEUTENANT THOMAS JEWETT

SERGEANT PRADO and I were examining our position that June morning. To our left, and about half a kilometer in advance of our line, was an isolated clump of small trees. "That grove should be a good place for a squad of machine gunners, if the Germans should attack," I said.

Sergeant Prado looked up. "I don't think so," he said; "I don't think that at all." He stood there stubbornly, shaking his head. I did not answer him immediately, as if I had not heard. "I think you'd better take several men to those trees and dig a line of trenches there," I said finally.

"I wouldn't do that, Lieutenant," he said. "That clump stands out like a sore thumb. The Germans are sure to figure we'll put men there, and shell hell out of it,—I been expecting that all morning."

"I'm sorry," I said; "but I think you understand my orders."

"Yes, sir," he said.

A few minutes later Prado and his men had wormed their way through the wheat, and with my field glasses I saw them enter the trees. Then, as I lowered my glasses, and was walking away, I heard one shell in the quiet air. I stopped, turned, and saw it strike short of the clump by ten yards. There was silence while I held my breath, and the German artillerymen recalculated their range. Then there came innumerable shells which twisted and whined in the air and exploded with terrific blasts among the trees. Geysers of dirt, leaves and broken branches sprang upward, and the trunks of the lashed trees bent this way and that, as if a hurricane were lost among them, and could not find its way out.

The shelling lasted for twenty minutes and then lifted as suddenly as it had begun. I ran through the wheat, terrified, regretting what my vanity had made me do; and when I reached the clump, the first objects I saw were the bodies of Alden, Geers and Carroll huddled together, their faces torn away, the tops of their skulls caved in. Lying across a fallen tree, his body ripped from belly to chin, was Sergeant Prado, while Leslie Jourdan stood upright looking down at his hand, from which the fingers had been shot away.

I leaned against a tree to keep from falling. "I didn't mean to do it," I said; "I didn't mean to . . ."

PRIVATE STEPHEN CARROLL

WHEN we reached the clump of trees, Sergeant Prado told us to dig in at once.

"I never heard anything so dumb," said Rowland Geers. "What's his idea in sending us out here?"

"Don't ask questions," said Sergeant Prado. "The government pays you your thirty bucks a month for doing what you're told, not for asking questions."

"Doesn't he know the Germans saw us crawling out here?" asked Les Jourdan. "Does he think the Germans are nit-wits?"

"You'd better start digging," said Sergeant Prado, "and save your conversation.—Write me a letter about it."

Then the first shell hit to the right of the clump, and we flattened against the earth. We lay there for a moment, hoping the shell had been a chance one, but in a few minutes the clump was full of shells. The young saplings swayed back and forth, while broken branches and leaves rained down on us. The ground seemed to explode under us, and the bursting shells and the whirling shrapnel made a noise like men playing different instruments in different keys.

Bob Alden was lying in the hollow with me. His eyes were turned so that only the whites showed. His lids kept fluttering down, and his lips puckered out. Then Rowland Geers crawled in the hollow with us. Bob turned and tried to speak to him and Geers leaned forward, his ear close to Bob's mouth, to catch the words, just as a shell landed squarely in the hole with us.

PRIVATE CARROLL HART

SERGEANT TIETJEN was with me that day we took the machine gun nest in Veuilly Wood. We found the crew all killed except one heavyset, bearded man, and he was badly wounded. Just as we came up, the bearded man reached inside his coat and fumbled. I thought he was going to throw a grenade, so I emptied my pistol into him. His arm came away from his coat with a jerking, irregular motion and his palm rested for a moment against his lips. Then the blood in his throat began to strangle him, and he made a gurgling, sighing sound. His eyes rolled back and his jaw fell open.

I went over and opened his palm to see what he had in it. It was the photograph of a little German girl. She was round-faced, and freckled, and her hair was curled, for the occasion, over her shoulders. "That must have been his daughter," said Sergeant Tietjen.

That night I couldn't sleep for thinking of that German soldier. I rolled and pitched about and toward daybreak Tietjen came over and lay down by me. "It's no use blaming yourself that way, fellow," he said; "anybody in the world would have thought he was going to throw a grenade."

PRIVATE WILLIAM ANDERSON

THERE I was, with my foot split open from heel to toe, and that doctor at the dressing station thought I'd stand for him sewing it up again without giving me anything to deaden the pain, except a couple of drinks of cognac. "I want some sort of an anesthetic!" I said, and I didn't say it in any uncertain voice, either.

A hospital corpsman tried to tell me that they were almost out of morphine, and that they were saving the little they had for officers. Did you ever hear anything so God damned silly? "What the hell!" I said. "Do you think officers are more delicate than anybody else? Why don't you let everybody draw straws for the morphine? Or make a rule that nobody except blue-eyed men over five feet eight inches are to get it?—Why don't you make some reasonable rule about it?"

Then the doctor said, "Take that man out and let him lay in the snow for a while. That'll deaden him up some."

"By God, I'd like to see you try that once!" I said; "I'd just like to see you try that!—I'll write a letter to the Major General Commandant; I'll write a letter to President Wilson—!"

Another doctor whose arms were bloody to his elbows said: "For Christ sake, give him a shot, if that will keep his mouth shut." Just when I was feeling numb I raised up and said to the first doctor: "And by God! you'd better do a first class job on it, too!" The bloody doctor laughed. "Are you still with us, 'Gentle Annie'?" he asked.

"———— Jack!" I said.

PRIVATE MARTIN DAILEY

I AWOKE in a hospital train. My eyes burned and chest ached and I could feel my leg throbbing with pain. From where I lay, I could catch a glimpse, occasionally, of the French countryside covered with poppies and mustard plants in bloom. I could hear the hum of voices and the clanging of engines when we stopped, for a while, at some station along the way. I lay back and closed my eyes again. There was a stench of disinfectant and dried blood in the coach, and that smell which comes from many men caged together.

Above me a man talked ceaselessly of Nebraska. His hand, hanging over his bunk, was grayish white and his nails were turning blue. He talked softly, in a slow voice. He wanted to talk a great deal, because he knew he was going to die before we reached the hospital. But there was nobody to listen to him. We lay there, mostly in silence, and thought of our own misery, like newly castrated sheep, too tired to find comfort in curses. We stared at the ceiling dumbly, or glanced out of the doors at the lovely countryside, now in full bloom.

PRIVATE HENRY DEMAREST

WHEN I arrived at the hospital, they gave me a hot bath and put a clean night shirt on me. Then an attendant wheeled me into the operating room, where the doctors worked night and day in shifts. I woke up, sometime later, between cool sheets that smelled of lavender.

The hospital had been a fine, private residence, in its time, and the room where my bed was placed had been the conservatory. Outside, I could see the park, with trees bending this way and that against the wind, like old women with capes spread out. I watched the trees and the rain for a long time. Then I understood for the first time those lines of Verlaine: "Tears fall in my heart like rain upon the town. . . ." I kept repeating them under my breath.

A long time afterward a doctor came by to look at me. I was crying, without making any sound. I knew what I was doing, but I didn't want to stop. "What's the matter with you, sonny?" he asked. "You haven't got anything to worry about. They'll make you another leg so good that nobody can tell it."

"I feel so grateful for being here," I said. "You see,

I was on the line for six months, and I expected to be killed every minute of that time. . . . I never expected to come out alive. And now to be here between clean sheets, with everybody so nice to me. . . ." I tried to stop crying, but I couldn't. . . . "This isn't very dignified," I said, "but I feel so happy, I'd like to go about licking people's hands . . ."

"All right," said the doctor, patting my head. "You go to sleep now. You tell me all about it when I come around to-morrow morning."

CORPORAL LLOYD SOMERVILLE

ALL the men in our ward were gas patients, and all of us were going to die. The nurses knew there was nothing that could be done for us, and most of the men realized it too. . . . Across the room, a man lay straining, and trying to breathe. Sweat rolled from his face and he caught his breath with a high, sucking sound. After each spell had passed he would lie back, exhausted, and make a bubbling noise with his lips, as if apologizing for disturbing the ward; because each time the man strained for his breath the other men unconsciously struggled with him; and when he lay back exhausted, we unclenched our fists, and relaxed a little ourselves. I thought, "That fellow reminds me of a broken-down soprano practicing her scales. . . ."

A man whose face was turning the color of wet cement leaned over his cot and began vomiting into a tin bucket. . . . Then the soprano tried again for a high note, and I knew that I couldn't stand it any longer. I beat the mattress with my fists, and my heart began racing, and I remembered the doctors had said my only chance lay in keeping calm and unexcited. . . .

The night nurse came over to me. She was fat and old,

and she walked on the sides of her feet like a tame bear. There was a purple birth-mark on her chin. She stood looking down at me helplessly.

"This is pretty amusing for you, isn't it?" I said. She didn't answer me, and I commenced laughing and crying and saying every filthy thing I had ever heard, but she bent over me quietly, and kissed me on the mouth. . . . "A big boy like you!" she said scornfully.—"Oh, I'd be ashamed: I really would! . . ." I took hold of her hand and held it tightly. I could feel my heart slowing down again. My toes uncurled and my legs began to relax. My legs were stiff and numb. They felt as if they had been beaten with a stick.

And so she stood above my bed trying to think of something to do for me. I turned my head and pressed my lips against her palm. I wanted her to know that I was not frightened any more. I looked into her eyes steadily, and smiled, and she smiled back at me. . . . "I know what will help you," she said, "and that's a good stiff shot of cognac." I said yes, I thought so too.

"You've drunk cognac before, haven't you?" she asked anxiously. "I don't want to be the one to give you your first drink. . . ."

PRIVATE LAWRENCE DICKSON

EARLY in June we took over a position in Belleau Wood just evacuated by the Sixth Regiment, who had made an attack that morning. There was a lot of salvage around and a number of letters which had been torn up and thrown away. I pieced a part of one letter together and read it, but I could never find the last pages. It was addressed to a man named Francis R. Toleman and it was the most interesting letter I ever read. I carried it around with me for a long time hoping that some day I'd meet this fellow Toleman, but I never did.

If he's alive to-day and reads this, I'd appreciate it if he would write and tell me if Jim and Milly ever made it up. I'd also like to know what in the world Alice Wilson did to make her own people turn against her that way.

PRIVATE NATHAN MOUNTAIN

WE could hear the motors droning above us, like a planing mill a long way off. Then there would be silence before the bomb came hissing down. At the first rush of the bomb, the column stopped in fright and the men braced themselves, hoping the aviator would miss the road that time. Then there would be a flash of light and an explosion, and we would walk around the shell hole, still smoking, and the dead men lying in it. The men would double time to catch up with the advance column, quarreling and jostling each other, carrying light packs only, their rifles slung over their shoulders.

Then Mamie, the galley mule, went nuts. She kicked and jumped forward and brayed steadily with a rasping sound. When Pig Iron Riggin tried to quiet her, she flattened her ears and snapped at his hand, her eyes rolling wildly. Finally she freed herself from her harness and came kicking and screaming down the road, the broken trace chain rattling behind her. She kicked furiously in circles for a minute and then she leaped the road and ran through the woods.

Afterward the planes, bolder now, came close to the

road and sprayed us with machine guns. We could see the flash of the guns, and the red tracer bullets looked like fireflies against the sky. . . . We lay flat in the road, hugging it, striving to become a part of the earth, while the bullets splattered around us.

"Old Mamie's having a spell of nerves," shouted Albert Hays, laughingly.

"Yes," I said.

At daybreak we reached Soissons and began the attack.

PRIVATE CHRISTIAN GEILS

"COME out of that shell hole!" said Sergeant Donohoe. "Come out.—Get going!"

"No," I said. "No." My body was jerking like a man with Saint Vitus's dance. My hands were trembling and my teeth kept clicking together.

"You bastard you!—You yellow bastard!" said Donohoe.

He began to jab at me with the barrel of his rifle. "Come out of there!" he said again.

"I'm not going any farther," I said. "I can't stand it any longer."

"You yellow bastard!" he repeated.

Lieutenant Fairbrother came up. "What's the matter here?" he asked.

I crawled out of the shell hole and stood facing them. I wanted to say something, but I couldn't. I began to back away slowly. "Stand still!" said the lieutenant, but I continued to back away.

"You yellow bastard!" said Sergeant Donohoe.

Then he raised his pistol and took aim at my head. "Stand still!" said Lieutenant Fairbrother.

I wanted to stand still.—I tried to stand still.—I kept

saying to myself: "If I don't stand still he'll shoot me as sure as the world! . . ." But I couldn't: I kept backing away. There was a silence for a moment. I could hear my teeth clicking together, playing a tune. "Stand still!" I said to myself. "Stand still, for Christ sake . . . he'll shoot you!" Then I turned and began to run, and at that instant I heard the crack of Sergeant Donohoe's pistol, and I fell in the mud, blood gushing out of my mouth.

PRIVATE MARK MUMFORD

WHEN Bernie Glass, Jakie Brauer and I jumped into the trench we didn't see anybody except a fat little German boy who was scared to death. He had been asleep in a dugout, and when we jumped down, with bayonets fixed, he ran out of the dugout and tried to climb over the side of the trench. Jakie caught him by the slack of the pants, and pulled him back and Bernie made a couple of passes at him with his bayonet, just to frighten him, and I'll say he did it! But when Jakie started talking to him in German, he calmed down a little.

He begged us to let him go free, but we told him we couldn't do that, as we had to take him prisoner, according to instructions from Captain Matlock. Then he said he'd rather be killed outright than taken prisoner, because the Americans chopped off the hands and feet of all their prisoners. Did you ever hear anything as foolish as that in your life? When Jakie told us what he had said, Bernie got sore for a minute. "Ask him where he got his dope," said Bernie. "Ask him who's been telling him such lies."

After Jakie had spoken to him again, he turned to

us and repeated his answer in English: "He says they told him that in training camp. He says everybody knows it. It's even in the newspapers."

"Well, the dirty little louse," said Bernie, "to say a thing like that when everybody knows it's the *Germans,* and not ourselves who do those things. Christ Almighty, that's what I call crust!"

Then he began to laugh: "I'll tell you what: Let's have some fun with him. Tell him, regulations say that when a man takes a prisoner, he's got to cut his initials on the prisoner's belly with a trench knife!"

"All right," said Jakie, and began to laugh.

When he got his face straight again, he told the German boy what Bernie had said, and I thought the boy was going to faint. He turned pale and lay with his cheek against the side of the trench, groaning. Then he unbuttoned his blouse and we saw that he was wearing a fine *Gott Mit Uns* belt. Jakie wanted it for a souvenir. He showed it to Bernie and told him he was going to take it, if one of us didn't want it, but Bernie said: "You can't do that: that would be stealing!"

Jakie said, "All right, then, I'll buy the belt offen him."

So he told the German boy he wanted his belt, and that he'd give him ten francs for it.

The German boy didn't answer him. I don't think he even heard Jakie, he was crying so and wringing his hands, thinking about how we were going to slice up his belly.

"Go on and take it, then!" said Bernie; "take it, if you want it!"

But when Jakie reached forward to unbuckle the belt, the little German boy screamed and cut his throat from ear to ear with a knife, which he had hidden under his tunic!

PRIVATE BERNARD GLASS

WHEN I saw Jakie Brauer fall, his arteries spouting blood against the side of the trench, like a chicken whose neck has been twisted off, I was so surprised that I stood like a fool while the German boy climbed over the side of the trench and started running. Then I came to myself and ran after him. I could have shot him easy, but that was too good for the bastard. . . . After the decent way we'd treated him: offering to *buy* his belt instead of taking it away from him, as we could have done without any trouble! He almost had me winded, but finally I caught him. I stuck my bayonet into him time after time. Then I hit him on the head with the butt of my rifle.

It was a treacherous, dirty trick to cut Jakie's throat that way. Jakie was the straightest man I ever knew and he wouldn't hurt a fly, if he could get out of it.—And to see him with his head almost cut off, and his eyes . . . It all goes to show that you can't trust a German. I know I never gave one an even break after that.

PRIVATE JOHN TOWNSEND

I WAS gassed about dusk, too late to be sent back to the dressing station, so Lieutenant Bartelstone told me to go into the deep dugout and get some sleep. He said he would have me sent to the rear the first thing in the morning.

Sometime in the night I was awakened by the sound of automatic rifles, and I heard shouting and cursing all down the line. I knew there was a raid coming off. I sat up and tried to open my eyes, but they had festered and stuck together. My chest felt tight and I was sick at my stomach. The firing increased and the shouting got nearer. I thought: "They're going to take these trenches! I'd better get out now, while I can!" I got up from the wire bunk and tried to grope my way out, but I kept stumbling over things and bumping my head; and at last I was so confused I didn't remember where the stairs were any more. I became frightened. I stood with my palms pressed against the wall and called softly: "Romano! . . . Halsey! . . ." But even as I called I knew that I was alone in the dugout.

There was shouting and firing directly over my head, and after that I heard running on the duckboards outside, and excited guttural words which I could not understand. The door of the dugout was opened and some one threw in a grenade. "Don't," I said, "don't. . . ."

I found the stairs at last and commenced climbing them carefully on my hands and knees until I reached the top step, and felt cold air in my face. I stood upright and raised my hands to show that I was not armed. I could not see, but I had a feeling that many men stood in front of me. . . . "I'm blind and helpless," I said; "please don't hurt me. . . ." There was silence, while I stood there waiting, my hands raised above my head; and then somebody jabbed a bayonet through my body and somebody clubbed me with the butt of a rifle and I fell down the stairs and into the dugout again.

PRIVATE WILBUR HALSEY

THE head nurse told us it was all right to go anywhere else in town, but to keep away from the Rue
Serpentine: If we went there our passes would be re-
voked, and we wouldn't get liberty again as long as we
remained in the hospital.

When we were outside in the sunshine, the first thing
Herb Merriam said to me was: "Where the hell is this
Rue Serpentine?" I laughed. "I don't know," I said;
"but let's go find it."

We looked around, but we couldn't locate it. Finally
we crossed the canal and went into a little café. We
ordered cognac. "Ask the waiter where it is," said Herb
Merriam. "Oh, I don't like to do that," I said. "Go on!"
said Herb. "Go on and ask him!"

When the waiter came around again, I spoke to him
in my best French: "Will you direct us, please, to the—"

But the waiter didn't hear me out. "Walk four blocks
east and turn to your right for the Rue Serpentine," he
said in a bored voice, without even raising his eyes from
the table.

Herb and I began to laugh. "Hurry up and finish
your drink," he said, "and let's get going."

We got back to the hospital an hour before supper time. Miss Mattson, the day nurse, was just going off duty. "Well, how did you boys like the Rue Serpentine?" she asked.

Herb began to blush, and so did I, both of us looking down at our feet.

"You better go downstairs and take a prophylactic," she said in a matter-of-fact voice. "Take the corridor to the right and knock on the first door."

PRIVATE HARRY WADDELL

THIS is the way it really happened: We were lying in a wood near Boissy, having just returned from the front where we had been in the line for ten days. Most of the men got soap and washed their clothes that afternoon, or wrote letters home, but one or two of us decided to go A.W.O.L. and see what the country looked like.

On the road, between two fields, I saw a girl watching a cow, brushing flies off its back with a willow stick. When she smiled at me, and made a sound with her mouth, I leaped the fence and came over to her. She looked at me, closing her eyes halfway, and laughed. Then she put her arms over her head and yawned, and as she did her breasts jumped at me like young rabbits. I walked over to her and put my hands on her thighs, and she came up to me with her hips and started to grind coffee. Then she pulled my head down against her breast, her eyes rolled back and we began to kiss. It was a hot day and her hair was plastered to her skull. Beads of perspiration were on her throat and lips and there was a smell of sweat and clover hay about her.

Then suddenly she shoved me away like she was

scared of something, and at the same moment I saw a man watching us over the hedge. The girl began to scream and hit me with the branch. I leaped the hedge and ran down the road, but the man came after me, shouting as he ran and waving a spade. Then other people joined in the chase, men and women armed with sticks and pitchforks. Finally they had me cornered in a pocket, and I stood still.

That was the way it really happened. So help me, God.

PRIVATE BENJAMIN HUNZINGER

I DIDN'T have the faintest idea of deserting: Nothing was farther from my thoughts, that night. But you see I'd met a barmaid in a café that afternoon, while on liberty in the village, and she had promised to meet me later down by the canal. Sergeant Howie was with me when I made the date, and testified for me at the trial, but it didn't do much good.

Well, after taps had sounded that night, I slipped out of camp and past the sentry on guard at the road. Annette (her name sounded something like that: I never did catch it exactly) was waiting for me, like she said she would. We walked arm in arm along the bank of the canal and sat down on the grass behind a thorn hedge in full bloom. I didn't know what to say, and she didn't know what to say, and neither would have understood the other, anyway. So we sat with our arms around each other, smelling the thorn flowers and listening to the canal swishing against reeds.

Then a moon came up and we stretched out on the grass. Later, we rolled under the hedge, and she let me get at her. We lay in each other's arms all night, but just before daybreak we parted, I going back to my company, and she standing with her back to the hedge, waving.

I cut across fields, hurrying to reach the bunk house before roll-call, but when I reached camp, my company was gone. I rolled my pack and hurried after them, trying to overtake them. When I did, ten days later, they were in action at St. Mihiel. My rifle was taken away and I was put under arrest, charged with desertion in face of the enemy. "You can't say that about me, by God!" I kept repeating. "I'm not a deserter. I didn't have any idea of deserting."

PRIVATE PLEZ YANCEY

WE were due a quiet sector for a change, and I'll say we got one. Behind us was the town of Pont-a-Mousson, in front of us the Moselle flowed, and on the other side of the river the Germans were dug in. The night we took over the trenches, the French told us the club rules and asked us not to violate them: In the morning the Germans could come down to the stream to swim, wash clothes, or gather fruit from the trees on their side of the river. In the afternoon they had to disappear and we were free to swim in the river, play games, or eat plums on *our* side. It worked nicely.

One morning the Germans left a note of apology telling us that we were going to be shelled that night at ten o'clock, and that the barrage would last for twenty minutes. Sure enough the barrage really came, but everybody had dropped back a thousand yards and turned in for the night, and no harm was done. We stayed there by the Moselle for twelve lovely days and then to our regret, we shoved on. But we had all learned one thing: If the common soldiers of each army could just get together by a river bank and talk things over calmly, no war could possibly last as long as a week.

LIEUTENANT ARCHIBALD SMITH

WHEN I entered the communication trench, I heard a pattering noise behind me, like somebody walking in his stocking feet. I turned quickly and Private Carter stood there, his rifle raised, with bayonet fixed, its point almost touching my breast. There was a strange, doped glitter in his eyes. His face was working and he made a piglike grunting noise in his throat. He pressed the bayonet against my belly and backed me to the wall of the trench. I looked about me, but there was nobody in sight; I listened with strained ears, but there was no sound on the duckboards.

"What do you want, Carter?" I asked as quietly as I could.

"You know!" he said. "You know you got it in for me!"

I shook my head. "You're mistaken," I answered. "You're very much mistaken, indeed, if you think that."

"Why don't you leave me alone?" he asked. "Why don't you take somebody else on patrol.—Why don't you let me go to sleep?"

Suddenly he began to yawn and a tired look came into his eyes. He swayed back and forth on his feet. I started to lower my hands and grasp the rifle, but he recovered, pressing me warningly with the bayonet, and my hands went up again. . . . Suddenly the whole thing struck me as absurd. I began to laugh. "Don't you see," I said, "I wanted to take you with me on patrol because I trust you, and consider you the best man in my platoon. That's all there is to it. I'm not trying to ride you. . . ."

He shook his head. "You got it in for me," he repeated.

"No!" I said. "No: you're wrong about that.—You're mistaken!"

"I got to get some sleep," he said. "I'm tired. I got to get some sleep. . . ."

"All right," I said. "Go back to the dugout and turn in. I'll see that you're not disturbed for twenty-four hours.—Go on back to the dugout and turn in, and we'll both forget this ever happened."

He shook his head again. His eyes blinked and almost closed. "You got it in for me," he repeated, as if he were reading from a book. Then, without haste, he pressed on the butt of his rifle and the bayonet entered my body slowly. Then he withdrew the bayonet and struck me quickly again and again. I fell to the duckboards and lay there in the mud. Above me Carter stood cleaning the blade with blue clay which he dug from the side of the trench.

PRIVATE EDWARD CARTER

O N Sunday night I was on a wiring party with
Sergeant Mooney. It was not my turn, but Lieutenant Smith said he wanted Mooney to take me along.
Monday morning I caught galley police, finishing up
just in time to go on patrol with Lieutenant Smith,
who had asked for me again. Tuesday morning was my
regular turn for guard duty, and Tuesday night I was
gas sentry at the dugout. Early Wednesday morning a
detail went to the rear to bring up rations, and Lieutenant Smith said I'd better go along because I knew
the roads. I had just got back and closed my eyes when
Sergeant Tietjen woke me up. "For Christ sake," I said.
"Get somebody else. I'm not the only man in this
platoon. I haven't had any sleep for a week."

"I can't help it," said Tietjen. "I know it looks lousy,
but Lieutenant Smith said I was to take you along."

"That bastard!" I said.—"Why has he got it in for
me? Why does he want to ride me all the time?"

"I don't know," said Tietjen. "I'm just telling you
what he said."

I got up again and went with the working party.
Coming back I was so tired and sleepy I could scarcely

hold my eyes open. I didn't wait for supper. I turned in, like I was, and was asleep before I got on the bunk good. . . . Then, almost immediately, somebody was standing over me, shaking me. I was not entirely awake, but I heard Corporal Brockett's voice coming from a long way off. "Eddie's pretty tired, Mr. Smith. He's been on a working party all day. Maybe you'd better take somebody else. . . ." And Lieutenant Smith's voice: "He'll be all right when he gets on his feet."

I opened my eyes and sat up, and Lieutenant Smith stood before me looking fresh and rested. "You bastard!" I thought. "You dirty bastard! . . ." I looked down at the floor and covered my face with my hands so that he couldn't see how much I hated him.

"We start at ten o'clock," he said. "We'll be out all night." Then he looked at his watch. "I've just got time to go to Headquarters and write a few letters before we start," he said. Then he laughed, patted me on the shoulder and went out. . . . "You bastard!" I thought.—"Why do you keep riding me?"

After he had gone, I sat there for a minute before making up my mind. Then I slipped out of the dugout and ran down the old communication trench which the French had abandoned, and which was partially filled up. I was waiting for him at the supply trench when he passed humming "La Paloma" under his breath. I had taken off my shoes, so as not to make a sound on the duckboards. I followed him for about three hundred yards, still undecided what to do, and then he turned and saw me. He tried to talk me out of it, but I pinned him to the side of the trench and stuck my bayonet in him until he quit breathing. After that I ran back as quickly as I could and was in the dugout, and asleep again, before the guard had completed his round, or before anybody had missed me.

PRIVATE EMIL AYRES

AT first I used to listen to Les Yawfitz and that fellow Nallett argue in the bunk house. They'd been to college, and they could talk on any subject that came up. But mostly they talked about war and how it was brought about by moneyed interests for its own selfish ends. They laugh at the idea that idealism or love of country had anything to do with war. It is brutal and degrading, they say, and fools who fight are pawns shoved about to serve the interest of others.

For a while I listened to them, and tried to argue the thing out in my mind. Then I quit thinking about it. If the things they say are really true, I don't want to know it. I'd go crazy and shoot myself, if I thought those things were true. . . . Unless a man does feel like that, I can't understand how he would be willing— how he would permit himself to—

So when they start talking now, I get up and leave the bunk house, or turn over to the wall and cover up my ears.

PRIVATE MARTIN APPLETON

DID you ever stand alone on a quiet night while the world trembled to the vibration of guns, and watch soundless light touch the horizon in unexpected places? Did you see a moon rise behind poplars and watch it climb upward, limb by laced limb, until it swung clear of the dead branches and into a quiet sky? . . . I have seen these things, and I tell you they are beautiful.

Then there are rockets, Very lights and flares (white, golden or green) that rise indolently to the air in long curves. Sometimes the rockets puff softly before your eyes into impersonal light that drifts down the wind; and sometimes they become stars of warm and beautiful coloring that burn purely for a moment, and expire before you can mark the instant of their annihilation.

I never see flares of Very lights floating over the trenches that I do not think of time and infinity, and the Creator of the universe; and that this war, and my despair, are, in His sight, as meaningless, and, no doubt, as remote as are the ascending and falling rockets to my finite mind.

PRIVATE LESLIE WESTMORE

SOMETHING kept saying to me, "If your gun should go off by accident and shoot you in the knee, your leg would become stiff, and the war would be over for you.—You would be lucky to get off that lightly."

I wouldn't listen to the voice whispering to me. "That would be a cowardly thing to do.—I'd never be able to hold my head up again.—I'd never be able to look people in the eyes," I thought. . . .

"If you were *blind,* now," the voice said again; "surely nobody could blame you if you went blind!— Think! Your uncle Frederick went blind and your grandmother lost her sight before she died. It runs in your family."

"That's very true," I said, "but Uncle Fred had cataracts, which could have been removed, and grandmother had good sight until she was past seventy-five."

"All right," said the voice. "Go ahead, then, if you'd rather be killed. . . . But you're a fool, that's all I can say!"

"I'd rather be killed than go blind," I said. "I'll take my chance on getting killed."

"You're lying," the voice said. "You know very well that you're lying. . . ."

I turned over on my bunk, thinking how comfortable this rest billet was compared with the dugouts in the line. In a few days we would be back at the front again. . . . "Try it!" said the voice.—"It isn't so bad. Your Uncle Fred was happy afterward, wasn't he? Think what a fuss everybody made over your grandmother, waiting on her hand and foot! . . . Shut your eyes and try it for a while! You'll see it isn't so bad. . . ."

"All right," I said, "but it's just for a minute."

I closed my eyes and said to myself: "Now I am blind." Then I opened them again, but when I did so, I couldn't see anything. . . . "This is ridiculous," I said. "There's nothing the matter with my eyes.—This is absurd." . . . "How do you know?" asked the voice. "Remember your grandmother and your Uncle Fred."

I jumped up, frightened. Everything was black in front of me as I walked forward and stumbled over some men playing black jack on the floor. "Look where you're going!" said Sergeant Howie. "Where the hell do you think you are?"

I stood there not moving. Then I felt Walt Rose standing up. I could hear his breathing and I knew he was peering at my face. . . . "Say, come here quick!" he said in an excited voice. I heard the squeak of Carter Atlas' bunk as he got up quickly. I heard the voices of

Walter Landt and Larry Dickson. I felt them closing in around me, but I stood there without saying anything.

"Can't you see us?" asked Walt Rose. "Can't you see us at all, Les?"

"No," I said. . . . "I'm totally blind." Then a feeling of relief came over me. I felt happier than I had in months. "The war is over for me," I said.

PRIVATE SYLVESTER WENDELL

C APTAIN MATLOCK was receiving a number of letters from the parents of men killed in action, so he decided to write to the next of kin of each dead man, as shown by his service record book, and he detailed me to gather the facts in each case and to write appropriate letters of condolence.

I sat there in the company office writing my letters while Steve Waller, the company clerk, made up his payroll. I gave every man a glorious, romantic death with appropriate last words, but after about the thirtieth letter, the lies I was telling began to gag me. I decided I'd tell the truth in at least one of the letters, and this is what I wrote:

"DEAR MADAM:
"Your son, Francis, died needlessly in Belleau Wood. You will be interested to hear that at the time of his death he was crawling with vermin and weak from diarrhea. His feet were swollen and rotten and they stank. He lived like a frightened animal, cold and hungry. Then, on June 6th, a piece of shrapnel hit him and he died in agony, slowly. You'd never believe that he could live three hours, but he did. He lived three

full hours screaming and cursing by turns. He had nothing to hold on to, you see: He had learned long ago that what he had been taught to believe by you, his mother, who loved him, under the meaningless names of honor, courage and patriotism, were all lies . . ."

I read that much of the letter to Steve Waller. He listened until I finished, his face without expression. Then he stretched himself a couple of times. "Let's go to the billet and see if we can talk the old woman into frying up a batch of eggs," he said.

I didn't say anything. I just sat there at the typewriter. "These frogs can beat the whole world when it comes to frying eggs," he said. . . . "Christ knows how they do it, but they're the nuts when it comes to cooking."

I got up then, and began to laugh, tearing into fragments the letter I had written.

"All right, Steve," I said; "all right; just as you say!"

PRIVATE RALPH BRUCKER

IF you boys want the real low-down on Fishmouth Terry, here it is: He's thirty-five years old and before war times he was a floor walker in a department store. His wife weighs two hundred pounds and in the picture I saw, she was wearing a low cut dress and was smelling a rose. Fishmouth calls her "Poochy," and she calls him "Terry-boy" and they write baby talk to each other in letters.

But wait, you haven't heard the worst about him. At night back of the line, he sits around in his underwear scratching his feet and eating Fig Newtons, and reads a book called "East Indian Love Lyrics." . . . But he's not a bad guy, really. Terry means well, but he hasn't got a whole lot of sense and when they begin to ride him at Divisional, it gets him excited and he takes it out on the company. He's always treated me right, and he's not a bad guy, no matter what you fellows think.—I guess I ought to know: I've been his orderly for eight months.

PRIVATE BYRON LONG

WE camped near Belleville that night and the next morning we had orders to go through a delousing plant situated in an open field. We took our clothes off outside the building, tied them together in a bundle with our identification cords, and the attendant put them in an oven to bake for an hour or so. Then we went through the plant in groups of fifty. It took all morning to run the battalion through and we had to stand around the field naked during that time, waiting to get our clothes back from the ovens.

After a while the sides of the field were lined with spectators, mostly women, who sat on the grass and watched, or ate their lunches, completely unconcerned. One old lady had brought a chair and some sewing with her. I walked over to where she was sitting, as naked as the day I entered this world. "They're going to delouse the First Battalion this afternoon," I said, "but if I were you ladies, I wouldn't wait. When you've seen a thousand naked men you've about seen them all.

"*Comment?*" said the old lady, smiling sweetly.

PRIVATE PHILIP WADSWORTH

MY chastity was one of the stock jokes in our company: replacement troops heard of it before they learned the names of their platoon commanders. I let them laugh, and minded my own business. It was useless, I knew, to try to make them see my viewpoint. I mention it now, merely because it accentuates the drollery of my ultimate fate.

Here's the way it came about: We were billeted in a French town to reorganize and replace equipment, and we were allowed considerable liberty during that time. Jesse Bogan, who was in my squad, suggested, one night, that we go to the Café de la Poste and split a bottle of wine. I had some letters to write; I wasn't keen about going; but he made such a point of it, I consented.

When we reached the café, it was full of soldiers, and there were a number of women sitting at the tables with them. As soon as Jesse and I came in, one of the women left the group she was with and joined us at our table. Sergeant Halligan and Hyman White and one or two others followed her, and tried to make her come back, but she put her arms around my neck and said, "No! No! This is my baby!" (I found out later the whole thing was arranged. Even Jesse Bogan, whom I trusted, was in on the joke.)

At last the men pretended to be sore with the woman, and went back to their table to enjoy the fun. Then Bogan got up and left, after a time, and the woman and I were alone at the table.

She asked me to go with her to her room, but I refused as politely as I could. I explained about Lucy Walters and how we had promised to remain pure, for each other, until we were married. The woman sat listening to me sympathetically. She said I was right. She said a girl rarely met a man with such a fine viewpoint. Then she commenced talking about the farm, near Tours, where she had been born, and how happy she had been there. She told me of her sweetheart, a boy from her village; how they, too, had loved each other, and planned marriage, and how he had been killed at the first battle of the Marne. She thought of him constantly, she said: She regretted, always, that he had died before he had consummated their love, or learned how rich and beautiful life could be. . . .

As she talked, I kept thinking: "My morals are absurd. I may be killed next week. I may never see Lucy again." The girl took my hand, and tears came into her eyes. "Everything is sad and a little mixed-up," I thought. "What difference can it make, one way or the other, if I go with this woman?"

Afterward I was ashamed of myself. I offered her twenty francs (I had no idea what the proper fee was in such cases), but she refused it. She clung to me and kissed me. She said I reminded her of the boy who had been killed at the Marne: he, too, had been very innocent. . . . And all the time she knew that she had diseased me.

Later I became alarmed and went to the dressing station. The doctor looked me over, laughed, and beckoned to the hospital corpsmen. I was courtmartialed for failing to report for a prophylactic and sent to this labor battalion. I have thought the matter over a thousand times, but I cannot understand, even yet, what there is about male chastity that is humorous, or why it repels and offends. The woman in the café got two hundred francs from my friends for seducing me. She reënacted the entire scene for them when she returned to the café: I was very clumsy and funny, I understand.

PRIVATE ALEX MARRO

W E were camped in a wood about ten kilometers from Nancy, and that afternoon Gene Merriam, our regimental runner, dropped by to see his brother, Herb. He had just been to Nancy with a message, and he was telling us all about it. "There's a house running wide open there," he said; "and you never saw such good-looking girls in your life. They've all got blonde hair, and they sit around on their big, fat cans dressed in lace kimonos, fanning themselves and eating pears. . . ."

After he had gone, Nate Mountain, Mart Passy and I kept talking of the various women we had known in our lives and wondering if we could get away with going A.W.O.L. that night. We put our money together, and it came to seventy-eight francs. We figured that should be enough for the three of us, even if it was a first-class house, so after roll-call had been taken, we slipped out.

Gene Merriam had given us exact directions. We didn't have much trouble in finding the place. Nate went up to the door and rang the bell and presently a big, raw-boned woman with a gray streak in her hair, opened it. But when she got a look at our dirty uniforms, she made motions for us to go away. Then she tried to shut the door again, but Nate was too quick for her. He got his foot in the crack and held it there. The woman began to chatter in a shrill voice, and to curse us in English.

Then an M.P., attracted by the noise, came up to see what it was all about. At first he said he was going to put us under arrest for being A.W.O.L., but Mart gave him fifty francs, and that put him in a good humor. "Who do you think you are?" he asked. "That house is for officers only: You got to wear captain's bars or better to get in there. . . ." Then he began to laugh. "Those whores are refined, sensitive girls. They wouldn't even unbutton their drawers for a bunch of grease-balls like you!" Then the M.P. stopped laughing and began to scowl. "Say, you get back to your outfit!" he said.—"You get the hell back before I change my mind and run you all in!"

PRIVATE JOHN McGILL

I WENT out on raiding parties time after time where every man except myself was killed or wounded. I have had my rifle splintered in my hands and twice my helmet was ripped through by shrapnel. I've had the buttons shot off my tunic and one time even the tape holding my identification discs was cut by machine gun bullets. And yet I never received a scratch, although I participated in all action with my company. I could go on citing you innumerable instances to show how lucky I am, but the strangest thing of all happened just after the battle of Soissons.

We were back in a wood reorganizing and waiting for stragglers to catch up. I needed a new mess-gear, my own having been destroyed with my pack, while strapped to my back during the fighting. (Another close shave, you see!) So I walked to a salvage pile and picked up a new mess-gear at random. When I got back to my tent and looked at it closely, I saw that it had my name, John McGill, cut into the metal with beautiful old English letters. That really was remarkable, wasn't it? . . . You can call it coincidence, if you like, but I know better. There are many things we cannot account for with all our laws of average and rules of chance. There are many strange forces working around us which we cannot understand. . . . The men in my company marveled at my luck. Before going over the top many of them would put their hands on my forehead, hoping thereby to become lucky themselves, but whatever the power that protected me, it never worked for any one else.

PRIVATE SIDNEY BORGSTEAD

WHEN Captain Matlock saw from my service record book that I had been a *couturier*, he, with his penchant for doing the inappropriate thing superbly, decided to transfer me to the galley and make a cook out of me. To him it seemed entirely logical that a man who had handled chiffons and lovely taffetas would be equally deft in the medium of beef carcasses and dehydrated potatoes.

At first I tried to prepare the rations as attractively as possible, but I soon found out nobody cared how the food was cooked. All they wanted was quantity, I mean, and positively hours before a meal was ready the men stood in line waiting hungrily and watching my every move. Of course it made me nervous and irritable! But the worst time of all was when we were dishing up the food; the men would stare at their rations and growl: not because of its quality, mind you (I could have understood and condoned that!), but merely because there wasn't *more* of it. (Heaven knows I couldn't cook any more food than Headquarters issued me: I'm not a magician, after all!) Then they would gobble it down like swine and get in line hoping for seconds.

PRIVATE SIDNEY BORGSTEAD

One day in Courcelles I was making a stew in a g.i. can, it was an hour before supper time but as I looked up I saw a line of men already forming. I became slightly hysterical, I'm afraid. I wanted to say to them, "Don't worry, little piglets, mamma pig will soon have supper ready!"

On a shelf to one side of the kitchen were some medicines and salves which Mike Olmstead, the mess sergeant, carried around with him for emergencies. I had a sudden idea and it set me to giggling. I opened the lid of the g.i. can and stirred it all into the stew.

When I was in bed that night, I thought, "Well, anyway, nobody will show up for breakfast and *that* will be a relief!" but when the guard woke me at five o'clock the next morning, the first thing I heard was somebody scraping his dirty mess-gear with a spoon. Then I heard men running and coughing and jostling for places in the line. When I came into the kitchen and started my fires, the line extended half a block. If there was anybody absent, you'd never be able to tell it with the naked eye.

I turned and ran. I didn't know where I was going, but I knew that I must get away. I bumped into Sergeant Olmstead in the doorway. He saw that I was profoundly upset and nervous. I stood beating him on the chest. "Let me pass!" I demanded; "Captain Matlock can get another cook, because I'm through. They can put me in jail—they can shoot me, if they want to, but I'm through for good!"

Sergeant Olmstead—he's really a good sort, but terribly dull—put his arm over my shoulder and stood patting my back. "Now, Cookie, don't get your bowels in an uproar," he said soothingly.

"Let me pass, please!" I said firmly.

"You wouldn't leave me flat, that way, would you?" he asked.

"Yes," I said.

He didn't try to detain me any longer. "Well, before you go, I want you to make some more of those apple turnovers. I never ate anything better in my life."

I looked at the man incredulously. "Did you think they were better than those peach pies I made for you in Saint Aignan?"

Sergeant Olmstead thought it over carefully and then decided to be diplomatic. "They were both so good that it's mighty hard to say which *was* the best," he said. I stood there uncertain and Sergeant Olmstead followed up his advantage. "How would the boys get along if they didn't have you to take care of them when they come back from the trenches?" he asked.

I laughed derisively. "They would be delighted!" I said. "They all hate my cooking."

Sergeant Olmstead shook his head seriously. "Don't you ever believe that," he said, "because you'll be wrong, if you do." Then he continued, "I heard some of our boys boasting in the café that we fed better than any company in the regiment. They said they sure felt sorry for those other companies."

"Are you really telling me the truth?" I asked.

"Sure. I'm telling it to you straight."

And because I'm a "dee" fool and haven't two brains to knock together, I let him exploit the better side of my nature, and I went back into the kitchen and started breakfast again.

PRIVATE ALLAN METHOT

MY poetry was beginning to attract attention when I enlisted, convinced of the beauty of war by the beauty of my own sonnets. Then months of training, drudgery and pain. But I could have stood the humiliation and the long hours of senseless work. I grew accustomed to those things and I could shake them off. It was the spiritual isolation that was unbearable.—Who was there to talk to? Who was there to understand me?—There was no one. . . . No one at all.

That sense of strangeness, of being alone! It closed around me more and more. I looked at my comrades with their dull, sheeplike faces. They asked nothing of life except sleep and food, or a drunken night in a brothel. A sense of revulsion came over me. Sodden, emotionless creatures, insensitive to beauty . . .

Then those nights on watch with Danny O'Leary, his eyes unlit by intelligence. He would stand there stupidly and stare at me, his heavy brows drawn together, his thick lips opened like an idiot's. I tried to talk to him, but it was useless. He lowered his eyes, as if ashamed of me, and stared at the duckboards, fumbling at his rifle. . . . "I wonder if we get paid when we get back this time?" he said.

I began to laugh. I walked to the end of the trench and stood looking at a gas flare burning with a green light in the north.—That sense of isolation! That sense of being alone among aliens! I climbed out of the trench and walked toward the German lines. I walked slowly, watching the flares and whispering the words of my poems, pausing and walking forward again.

"Soon a hand will stretch out and jerk me off my feet," I thought, "and I shall lie broken against this broken earth. . . . Soon a foot, shaped like infinity, will step upon my frail skull, and crush it!"

PRIVATE DANNY O'LEARY

I WOULD like you to see me now, Allan Methot: I would like you to see what you have created!—For you did create me more completely than the drunken longshoreman from whose loins I once issued.

I was so gross, so stupid; and then you came along.— How did you know? How could you look through layer upon layer until you saw the faint spark that was hidden in me? . . . Do you remember the nights on watch together when you recited Shelley and Wordsworth?— Your voice cadencing the words was the most beautiful thing I had ever heard. I wanted to speak to you, to tell you that I understood, to let you know your faith in me would not be wasted, but I dared not.—I could not think of you as a human being like myself, or the other men of the company. . . . I thought of you as some one so much finer than we that I would stand dumb in your presence, wishing that a German would jump into the trench to kill you, so that I might put my body between you and the bullet. . . . I would stand there fumbling my rifle, hoping that you would speak the beautiful lines forever. . . . "I will learn to read!" I thought. "When war is over, I will learn to read! . . ."

PRIVATE DANNY O'LEARY

Where are you now, Allan? I want you to see me.— Your friendship was not wasted; your faith has been justified. . . . Where are you, great heart? . . . Why don't you answer me?

PRIVATE JEREMIAH EASTON

AFTER we had taken over our position, Captain Matlock sent me back to the cross-roads, a kilometer to the rear, to guide in the wagon train. The woods were filled with artillery and troops were moving up all along the line. "This is going to be something big," I thought. "It's no little trench raid, this time!"

Then, at dusk, the German planes came over and began bombing the roads and wood. They would swoop down suddenly and open up with machine guns and then dart up again out of range. At nine o'clock it was pitch dark, and at ten it began to rain. The rain fell in torrents and a cold wind swirled it about, but still the men came on, thousands and thousands of them. When it lightened I could see them distinctly, their heads lowered to the blinding rain, pushing forward slowly down the roads and through the woods, disappearing like giant snakes into the communication trenches that emptied into the line. . . . "This is really going to be something big," I said. "No little penny fight this time."

Then toward morning the rain stopped and the first of the guns opened. Instantly a thousand guns were firing in a roaring, flashing semi-circle, and a thousand shells were flying through the air and exploding in the German lines. The barrage lasted for three hours and then, just at daybreak, it lifted. From where I was, I could see our men going over, the early light gleaming against fixed bayonets. But there was little for them to do, for there was nothing left of the German trenches or the surrounding terrain: Not a tree, not a blade of grass. Nothing living. Nothing at all. The dead lay thick in the trenches, in strange and twisted groups. . . . "There's nothing living left," I thought; "nothing at all!"

And then from a demolished pill-box a man crawled out of wreckage. His jaw was partially shot away, and hung down, but he held up the pendulous bone with his hand, when he saw us, and made a frightened, conciliatory sound.

PRIVATE WILLIAM MULCAHEY

WE crept toward the machine gun nest, each man with a grenade in his hand ready to throw, crawling slowly, hugging the earth, trying not to ripple the dense weeds. Then the Germans discovered us and opened fire, shouting excitedly.

We jumped up from the ground and hurled our grenades and ran forward firing our rifles, our bayonets fixed for action. . . . Then something hit me squarely and I fell into the weeds again. Excited firing broke out all along the line. There were curses and shouts and then, a few minutes later, everything was quiet except Pete Stafford dragging himself back toward our line on his elbows and saying over and over: "My leg's broke!—My leg's broke! . . ."

I raised my head and tried to speak to Pete, but the ground tilted up and then began spinning around like a roulette wheel. I lay back in the weeds again.—"I'll never know how the war comes out," I thought. "I'll never know, now, whether the Germans win or not."

SERGEANT JULIUS PELTON

O N the afternoon of the fourth day we fell back to the edge of the wood and dug in, and the First Battalion passed over our heads and continued the attack. In front of us stretched a wheat field and a wrecked farmhouse, and beyond that the wood started again. The wood before us seemed intact and unhurt, but the wood in which we lay was littered with toppling trees and torn branches, still green. To our left was a gravel pit, long abandoned, with one narrow opening; and back of that a ravine ran straight for a hundred yards and stopped blindly against a bank of clay.

From where I was lying I could see the gravel pit, with Johnny Citron on guard at the gap, watching the twenty-two prisoners we had taken that day. Then Captain Matlock came over to me. "What'll we do with them, sergeant?" he asked.

"I don't know, sir," I said.

"The easiest thing would be to train a machine gun on the gravel pit," he added; "that would be the simplest way."

"Yes, sir," I answered, and laughed, not taking him seriously.

"No," he said after a minute's thought; "the gap is too narrow and the sides are dug in so it would be pretty hard for the gunners. . . ."

I seen then that he was not joking.

"We'd better take them into the ravine and do it there," he said. . . .

I listened to what he was saying, keeping my mouth shut, but while he was talking I kept thinking: "I've been in the service since I was a kid eighteen years old. I've seen a lot of things that would turn an ordinary man's stomach. I guess I shouldn't be particular now. . . . But this is raw!—This is the rawest thing I ever heard of!"

When Captain Matlock stopped talking, I saluted him. "Yes, sir," I said.

"You'd better take Corporal Foster and his automatic rifle squad. I think Foster is the right man to do it."

"Yes, sir," I said; "yes, sir; I think he is."

"You'd better tell Foster to get it over with before dark."

"Yes, sir," I said.

Later, when I was talking to Foster, I felt ashamed. . . . "Christ! but this is raw," I thought. . . . "Christ! but this is the rawest thing I ever heard of!" . . . Then I remembered what my old drill sergeant had told me in boot camp, twenty years before. "Soldiers ain't supposed to think," he said; "the theory is, if they could think, they wouldn't be soldiers. Soldiers are supposed to do what they are told, and leave thinking to their superior officers."

"Well," I said to myself, "I guess it's none of my business. I guess I'm here to carry out instructions." Then I walked to where Foster was and repeated Captain Matlock's orders.

CORPORAL CLARENCE FOSTER

"THAT'S an old trick," I said. "I remember reading about it in the papers back home before I enlisted: The Germans send men over in droves, to give themselves up, and after a while there are more prisoners back of the line than soldiers. Then the Germans make an attack, which is a signal for the prisoners to overpower their guards and come up from the rear.— It's an old gag!" I said; "and it generally works. Those Prussians are smart babies, don't ever forget that!— They've pulled that trick on the French time and time again. . . . I'm surprised you never heard about it, sergeant," I said.

"I've heard a lot of hooey in my time," he answered.

"Well, this is straight dope," I said. "I've seen it all written up in the newspapers."

"Do you believe all the tripe you read in newspapers?" asked Sergeant Pelton.

"Well, I believe *that!*" I said; "I wouldn't put anything dirty past a German."

Sergeant Pelton began to laugh. "Captain Matlock said you were the right man for the job."

"I take his confidence in me as a compliment," I

answered. . . . "Christ almighty!—This is *war!* . . .
What did you think it was? A Sunday-school picnic? . . .
Take these Germans now.—Burning churches and dash-
ing out the brains of innocent babies.—You've got to
fight fire with fire," I said. "This is the only sort of
treatment a German can understand . . ."

Sergeant Pelton walked away. "All right. Be ready in
half an hour," he said. "Let's get it over quick." Then
I walked back to the trench where my squad was and
told them Captain Matlock's orders. I realized a great
many people, who did not understand the necessity for
such an act, would censure Captain Matlock for shooting prisoners, but under the circumstances, there was
no other way out. I expected an argument from Walt
Drury and that sea-lawyer, Bill Nugent, and I got it.
"Don't tell me," I said; "if the arrangement don't suit
you, tell your troubles to Captain Matlock!"

"He wouldn't dare do a thing like that," repeated
Nugent; "not a dirty thing like that . . ."

"What do you birds think this is?" I asked. "This is
war! . . . Why didn't you bring along your dolls and
dishes to play with! . . ."

PRIVATE WALTER DRURY

CORPORAL FOSTER told us to load our rifles and go to the gravel pit. There were some prisoners there, and Captain Matlock had ordered us to take them into the ravine, and shoot them. . . . "I won't do it!" I said.—"I might kill a man defending my own life, but to shoot a human being in cold blood . . . I won't do that!—I won't do it!" I said. . . .

"You'll do what the Captain says or you'll get a courtmartial. Then they'll stand you up and shoot you too.—Maybe you'd like that!"

"I won't do it!" I said.

"All right," said Corporal Foster. "Use your own judgment, but don't say I didn't warn you."

Then we took our rifles and walked to the gravel pit. There were about two dozen prisoners, mostly young boys with fine, yellow fuzz on their faces. They huddled together in the center of the pit, their eyes rolling nervously, and spoke to one another in soft, frightened voices, their necks bending forward, as if too frail to support the heavy helmets they wore. They looked sick and hungry. Their uniforms were threadbare and torn, and caked with mud, and their bare toes protruded through crevices in their boots. Some were already wounded and weak from loss of blood, and could hardly stand alone, swaying back and forth unsteadily.

Then suddenly my own knees got weak. "No," I said; "no.—I won't do it. . . ." Corporal Foster was getting the prisoners lined up in single file, swearing angrily and waving his hands about. . . . "Why don't I refuse to do this?" I thought. "Why don't all of us refuse? If enough of us refuse, what can they do about it? . . ." Then I saw the truth clearly: "We're prisoners too: We're all prisoners . . . No!" I said. "I won't do it!"

Then I threw my rifle away, turned and ran stumbling through the woods. I heard Corporal Foster calling to me to come back; I heard Dick Mundy and Bill Nugent shouting, but I ran on and on, dodging behind trees and falling into shell holes, hiding and trembling and then running forward again. Finally I came to an old barn and hid there behind a pile of refuse and tried to think of what I had done. I had no friends to shield me. I could not speak French. I didn't have a chance. I would be picked up by the military police sooner or later and tried as a deserter. That was inevitable, I knew. . . . "Better give myself up and get it over with," I decided; "maybe I'll get off with twenty years.—Twenty years isn't such a long time." I thought, "I'll only be forty-two, when I come out, and I can start life all over again. . . ."

PRIVATE CHARLES GORDON

WHEN we got the prisoners lined up, and had started them out of the pit, Walt Drury made a funny noise, threw his rifle away and ran through the woods. . . . "Walt!" I called.—"Walt!"

"Let him alone," said Corporal Foster, "he'll get his later."

Then the prisoners came out of the pit stolidly with their heads lowered, neither looking to the right nor the left. The wood had been raked by artillery fire, but recently, and the leaves that clung to the shattered trees and the pendent branches were still green. In places the trunks of the trees had been scored by shrapnel, leaving strips of bark, gnawed-at and limp, dangling in the wind; leaving the whitish skin of the trees exposed, with sap draining slowly . . .

"Come on," said Foster. "Come on. Let's get going before dark."

We picked our way through the wrecked wood, lifting aside the trailing branches, kicking with our boots the leaves that had rained down and made a green carpet. When we reached the entrance to the ravine, the prisoners drew back, frightened, and began to talk excitedly amongst themselves, then, glancing apprehensively over their shoulders, they entered, one by one, and huddled against the far bank.

One of the prisoners had very blue eyes and didn't seem frightened at all. He began to talk to his comrades, smiling and shaking his head. I couldn't understand what he was saying, but I had an idea he was telling them not to worry because there was nothing to fear. . . . "These men are wearing different uniforms and they speak a different language, but they are made out of the same flesh and blood that we are," I imagined him saying. "There's nothing to fear. They aren't going to hurt us."

Suddenly the blue-eyed man looked at me and smiled, and before I knew what I was doing, I smiled back at him. Then Sergeant Pelton gave the signal to fire and the rifles began cracking and spraying bullets from side to side. I took steady aim at the blue-eyed man. For some reason I wanted him to be killed instantly. He bent double, clutched his belly with his hands and said, "Oh! . . . Oh!" like a boy who has eaten green plums. Then he raised his hands in the air, and I saw that most of his fingers were shot away and were dripping blood like water running out of a leaky fawcet. "Oh! . . . Oh!" he kept saying in an amazed voice. . . . "Oh! Oh! Oh!" Then he turned around three times and fell on his back, his head lower than his feet, blood flowing from his belly, insistently, like a tide, across his mud-caked tunic: staining his throat and his face. Twice more he jerked his hands upward and twice he made that soft, shocked sound. Then his hands and his eyelids quit twitching.

I stood there spraying the bullets from side to side in accordance with instructions. . . . "Everything I was ever taught to believe about mercy, justice and virtue is a lie," I thought. . . . "But the biggest lie of all are the words 'God is Love.' That is really the most terrible lie that man ever thought of."

PRIVATE ROGER INABINETT

WHEN the last prisoner quit kicking, my squad went out of the ravine and back to their trench. I stepped behind a fallen tree, and they passed on ahead without missing me. For a while I could hear them moving through the wood, rustling the leaves with their feet, but after a time everything was quiet again. Then I went back and began going through the pockets of the dead men, but it was hardly worth the trouble. Most of them had paper marks and a few metal coins with square holes punched in them. I put these in my pocket. They might have some value: I didn't know. Then there were a lot of letters and photographs which I tore up and threw on a pile. Some of the men were wearing regimental rings which I took off their fingers—they're worth three or four francs each—and one had a fine, hand-carved cigarette lighter, shaped like a canteen, but there wasn't much of anything else.

What I was really looking for were Iron Crosses. They're worth real money back in the S.O.S. They make fine souvenirs and the boys buy them to send back to their sweethearts. Sometimes they bring as much as 150 francs each. The squareheads generally wear them pinned to their undershirts, under their tunics, where they won't show. I looked over every man carefully, but if there was a single decoration among those prisoners, I couldn't find it.

When I was almost through, I looked up and saw Sergeant Pelton watching me steadily, without moving his eyes.

"I'm looking for Iron Crosses," I said.

Then he caught me by the collar and pulled me up. "Put that stuff back," he said.

"What's the sense in that, sarge?" I asked. "We got more right to it than anybody else. If we don't get it, somebody else will." Then I took the cigarette lighter and offered it to him. "Here, you can have this, if you want it," I said.

For a moment I thought he was going to hit me, but he thought better of it. He turned me loose suddenly and walked away. "Get on back to your squad," he said.

"All right," I said; "if that's the way you feel about it, it's all right by me.—But there's no use your getting sore."

"Get on back to your squad!" he said.

PRIVATE RICHARD MUNDY

I DECIDED to take my rifle apart and clean it thoroughly. I didn't want to think about those prisoners any more, but as I sat there with my squad in the shallow trench, with the rifle parts scattered about me, I couldn't help thinking about them. Corporal Foster was opening cans of monkey meat with a bayonet and Roger Inabinett divided the meat and the hardtack into eight equal parts.

Charlie Gordon got out his harmonica and began to play a lively tune, but Everett Qualls stopped him. Then Foster passed out the rations and each man took his share. At sight of the food, Bill Nugent took sick. He went to the edge of the trench and vomited. When he came back his face was white. Jimmy Wade had a canteen of cognac which he passed over to him and Bill took a big swig of it, but immediately he got up and vomited again. Then he lay stretched out and trembled.

"What's the matter with you, Bill?" asked Foster.

"Nothing," he said.

"They've pulled that trick on the French a thousand times, and got away with it, too!" said Foster. "These

Germans are smart hombres. You got to watch them all the time."

Ahead of us, in the wheat field, the rays of the late sun lay flat on the trampled grain, but in the wood it was almost dark. Inabinett was playing with a cigarette lighter he had found in the wood. He kept snapping it with a clicking sound. "All it needs is a new flint," he said. "It'll be as good as new with another flint."

I put my rifle back together and rubbed the butt with oil. I kept seeing those prisoners falling and rising to their knees and falling again. I walked to the end of the trench and looked over the top. A long way ahead was the sound of rifle fire and to the west there was intermittent shelling, but here, in the wood, everything was calm and peaceful. "You wouldn't know we were in the war at all," I thought.

Then I had an irresistible desire to go to the ravine and look at the prisoners again. I climbed out of the trench quickly, before anybody knew what I was going to do. . . .

The prisoners lay where we had left them, face upward mostly, twisted in grotesque knots like angleworms in a can, their pockets turned outward and rifled, their tunics unbuttoned and flung wide. I stood looking at them for a while, silent, feeling no emotion at all. Then the limb of a tree that grew at the edge of the ravine swayed forward and fell, and a wedge of late sunlight filtered through the trees and across the faces of the dead men. . . . Deep in the wood a bird uttered one frightened note and stopped suddenly, remembering. A peculiar feeling that I could not understand came over me. I fell to the ground and pressed my face into the fallen leaves. . . . "I'll never hurt anything again as long as I live," I said. . . . "Never again, as long as I live. . . . Never! . . . Never! . . . Never! . . ."

PRIVATE HOWARD NETTLETON

"I DON'T want to hear any more out of you," said Sergeant Dunning. "Captain Matlock has passed an order that everybody, except the men detailed to repair roads, are to go to church, and like it, and by God! you'd better do it, if you know what's good for you!— Don't think you can get away with anything, either, because Pig Iron Riggin is going to be there with a roster, and check every man off." Well, that broke up the black jack game. "It looks like they could leave a man alone on Sunday morning back of the line," said Archie Lemon; "it looks like they could, at least, do that."

"Come on, let's get it over with," said Vester Wendell. "Once more won't hurt anybody."

Bob Nalls spoke up: "If I have to listen again to that chaplain praying to God to spare all the American Galahads and destroy their ungodly enemies, I'm going to get up and say: 'Who was telling you? Where do you get all this inside information? . . .' If he does that again, I'm going to ask him if he doesn't know that the Germans are praying too.—'Let's be logical about this thing,' I'm going to say; 'Let's pick out different Gods to pray to. It seems silly for both sides to be praying to the same one! . . .' "

"Come on! Come on!" said Sergeant Dunning. "You birds give me a pain.—You're not going to say anything at all: You're going to do just what you're told, and you're going to pray and sing hymns and like it!— Come on," he said, "let's get going."

PRIVATE HARLAND PERRY

A MAN from the Fifteenth Field Artillery named Charlie Cantwell told me this story. It seems he had been gassed, and was lying with his eyes bandaged, when the man next him reached over and woke him. He thought, at the time, that it was about three o'clock in the morning, but he didn't know for sure.

Then, according to Charlie's story, his neighbor said that he was going to die. Charlie couldn't see him, of course, because of his bandaged eyes, but he had a feeling that the man was about twenty-five years old, with brown eyes, black curly hair and a cleft in his chin. Charlie scoffed at the idea of the other man dying, but the man insisted that he was. Then he asked Charlie if he thought he, Charlie, was going to get well, and Charlie said yes, he was pretty sure of it. So the man reached under his pillow (I don't know how Charlie knew all this, if he had his eyes bandaged like he said) and pulled out a roll of bills that would choke a cow. "Here are ten thousand francs," the man said. "Spend it all for a good time." Charlie took the money and slipped it under his mattress. "Spend it foolishly," the man said; "spend as much of it on women as possible." Charlie promised to do that, and toward morning the man died. . . .

Well, that's the way Charlie told me the story, and personally I don't give one good God damn whether you believe it or not! It's no skin off my back-side.— All I know is what Charlie told me, and that he did have ten thousand francs, and that we spent hell out of the money after we got well enough to go on liberty into the town.

PRIVATE ALBERT NALLETT

BEFORE the company came to France, they were stationed in the tropics and while there they picked up Tommy, the company mascot. I don't know exactly what he was, but he looked more like a 'coon than anything else. Sergeant Halligan said the natives of Honduras called them ant bears. I don't know about that, but I do know Tommy had more sense than Captain Matlock and all his officers put together. We'd all be asleep in a dugout and some sentinel would sniff the air, get excited and turn in the gas alarm. Then the men would sit around with their gas masks on until their heads ached with the strain. Finally I tumbled to the fact that Tommy would lie curled up asleep through the excitement, if the alarm was false, but if there really was gas about, he didn't need a sentinel to tell him: He'd go dig a hole in the ground and pile dirt up around his snout. After I found that out, I never paid any attention to the alarms unless Tommy said it was all right. I never got gassed, either.

Tommy was very fond of condensed milk and Mike Olmstead, the mess sergeant, used to feed it to him. One time after St. Mihiel, the rolling kitchen got lost from the company for two days. Captain Matlock sent out a dozen runners to try to locate it, but none of them could. Then I unchained Tommy and said to him: "Listen, Tommy!—Find Mike!—Condensed milk! . . . Mike's got condensed milk for you!" Tommy jumped off my shoulder and took out through the woods, straight ahead, his tail twitching with excitement. I thought he was wrong that time, myself, but I followed him, anyway, and in fifteen minutes he had located the kitchen and was climbing up Mike's leg and nuzzling his cheek. It turned out that Mike and his kitchen had passed us in the night, on the road, and was several kilometers in *advance* of our line, but Captain Matlock hadn't sent any runners in that direction. When Mike came back with his kitchen and reported where he had been, Captain Matlock said that that was impossible. He said Mike couldn't possibly have passed us in the night without somebody hearing him.

I scratched Tommy's belly, which was full of condensed milk, and winked and Tommy drew back his lips and rubbed his snout, which is as close as he can come to giving anybody the horse-laugh.

PRIVATE ROBERT NALLS

FOLLOWING the fighting at St. Mihiel, we were billeted in Blenod-les-Toul with an old French couple. They had had an only son, a boy named René, who had been killed early in the war, and they were constantly finding points in common between us and him. I had brown eyes, and René's eyes had also been brown; René had had long, slender fingers, and Sam Quillin's fingers were also long and slender. They found resemblances to René in every one: Jerry Blandford because his teeth were even and white; Roger Jones for his thick, curling hair and Frank Halligan because of the trick he had of closing his eyes and throwing back his head when he laughed. Their lives centered around their dead son. They talked about him constantly; they thought of nothing else.

After his death, the French government had sent them a small copper plaque showing in bas-relief the heroic face of a woman surrounded by a wreath of laurel, and under the woman's face were the words, "Slain on the Field of Honor." It was not an unusual decoration. It was the sort of thing that a Government would send to the next of kin of all men killed in action, but the old couple attached great importance to it. In one corner of the room they had built a tiny shelf for the medal and its case, and underneath it the old woman had fixed up an altar with two candles that burned day and night. Often the old woman would sit for a long time silent before the altar, her hands twisted and old, resting her knees. Then she would go back and scrub her pans, or walk outside to the barn and look at her cow.

We remained in Blenod for five days, and then one night we got orders to move. The old couple had become very friendly with us by that time. They walked with us to the place of assembly, offering to carry our rifles or our packs. Then they stood in the muddy road, the September wind blowing against them strongly, crossing themselves and asking God to bring us all safely back.

A few weeks later, when we were miles away from Blenod, I saw the copper plaque again: It rolled out of Bernie Glass's kit bag while he was shaving one day. He picked it up quickly, but he knew that I had seen it.

"How could you do it, Bernie?" I asked; "how could you do a thing like that?"

"I don't know that it's any of your business," said Bernie, "but I thought it would make a good souvenir to take home."

I never returned to Blenod, and I never saw that old couple again, but somehow I wish they knew that I am ashamed of the whole human race.

PRIVATE OSWALD POLLARD

HERE'S a funny thing: In September a fellow named Fallon out of the fourth platoon went off his nut. He got up on the parapet of the trench, during a barrage, and nobody could coax him in. We tried to talk to him, to make him come back, but he wouldn't do it. "I want to get shot," he kept saying; "I know perfectly well what I'm doing. I want to get shot—I'm committing suicide, you see!"

Then Pig Iron Riggin took out his pistol and leveled it at this fellow Fallon's head. "If you don't quit committing suicide, I'll kill you as sure as I'm a foot high!" he said. Instantly Fallon turned white and began to whimper. He jumped into the trench and got down upon his knees. "Don't!" he said. "Don't kill me—please . . ."

PRIVATE MARTIN PASSY

THE boys all wondered about my lack of fear. I didn't let on, but deep in my heart I knew I didn't deserve any credit like Harold Dresser or Sergeant Tietjen for the things I did. At first I used to worry about the war and getting killed, and then that day in Baltimore, while on leave, I saw a sign on a door:

MADAME BONATURA

THE SEEREST OF THE EAST

Tells Your Past, Present and Future

I went into her parlor and we sat there talking for a time. Then she lowered the blinds and lighted a tiny lamp that shone on her face, and looked into a crystal ball. A funny expression came into her eyes and she began to twitch. Then she started talking in a sleepy voice, telling me the names of my two brothers, the number of my company and many other things. Finally she seemed to get excited: she began to talk hoarsely. "Ask me a question, and I will answer it," she said.

"Well," I thought, "I might as well know once and for all and get it off my mind. . . ."

"Ask me a question—any question you want," she said.

"Will you really tell me the truth, even if the answer is bad?" I asked.

"Yes," she said.

"Then tell me if I will be killed in the war."

Madame Bonatura looked into the crystal ball for a long time before answering. I wanted to say, "No!— Don't tell me! Don't answer!" but I wouldn't do it. "I might as well know the truth now, as any time," I thought. Finally the Madam began to speak, and I caught my breath again. "You will not be killed, or even wounded," she said. "You will be returned to those you love, will marry the girl of your choice and live happily ever after."

So you see I didn't really deserve all the credit I got. I wasn't any braver than anybody else and besides that I knew all the time that nothing could possibly happen to me, no matter what I did.

PRIVATE LEO HASTINGS

ALL that morning the German sniper shot at me. I would stick my head up, or walk across the open space, and there would come a faint ping and a bullet would pass harmlessly over my head. Then I would stop in my tracks and stand there a full two seconds, or suddenly take a step backwards and a step to the side. I would walk that way up and down the parapet of the trench laughing at the sniper. I knew I had him so sore at me that he was almost ready to break down and cry. I'd shot with telescopic sights myself and I knew no sniper in the world could hit a man who varied his stride as I did, unless the sniper could figure out in advance the man's system and he's got about as much chance of doing that as he has of breaking the bank at Monte Carlo.

"I'll stand here and let him take pot shots at me all day," I said; "he can't hit me in a thousand years.— See, as I stand now, he's got me covered. But wait! He's got to figure his distance, taking an angle between that dead tree and the farmhouse, probably. Now he's got it all doped out. He's taking his windage and calculating elevation. Now he's all ready to plug me, but by stepping one pace to the right, or doing this clog step, I upset all his calculations. See," I said, "there goes his bullet two feet to the right. He can't hit me to save his neck," I said.

PRIVATE SILAS PULLMAN

ONLY a few minutes more and we'll be going over. I can hear my watch ticking—ticking. This silence is worse than shelling. . . . I've never been under fire before: I don't know whether I can stand it or not.— This isn't the way I thought it was going to be.—I want to turn and run. I'm yellow, I guess. . . . The other men aren't frightened at all. They just stand there holding their rifles, cracking jokes. . . . Maybe they're as frightened as I am. How do I know? How can I tell what's going on in their minds. . . . Sergeant Mooney is speaking to me: "See that your bayonet is fastened tight," he says.—I nod my head.—I don't dare speak. . . . Oh, Christ! don't let anybody see how frightened I am.—Don't let them see, please! . . . I won't think about it any more. I'll think about something else.

Lieutenant Jewett has given the signal. Sergeant Mooney is climbing out of the trench. "All right, over you go!" he says. We're all climbing out. Now we're walking forward slowly.—Why don't the Germans open fire? They know we're coming over. They can see us.— For Christ sake, start firing! We're not fooling you! Go ahead: shoot at us! . . .

Down! Down!—Down on your belly, you fool! Do you want to be bumped off?—The Germans have opened up. We're down close to the ground, crawling; crawling inch by inch. They haven't got our range yet. . . . "Our orders are to crawl until we're fifty yards from their trenches, and then dash forward and attack." —Just dash forward, and attack.—That's very simple.— Just attack. . . .

They've got our range now. Corporal Brockett is hit in the shoulder. He's crawling for a shell hole.—Now he's in it. He's safe from the machine guns' bullets there. . . . Why doesn't he stop twisting about? That won't help matters.—That won't do any good. . . .

The bullets are plowing the dirt a foot from my head. Down closer! Hug the ground closer, you fool! . . . Mart Appleton and Luke Janoff are hit now. They fell at the same instant, almost. They lay there quietly, neither of them moving. . . . Now the man next to me is hit. Who is he? . . . His name is Les Yawfitz, I think. He stands up and then falls down. He's shot in the face. Blood is running down his face and into his mouth. He's making a choking sound and is crawling about like an ant. He can't see where he's going. Why don't you lie still. . . . That seems the sensible thing to do: You can't see where you're going, you know.

We're closer to the trenches. . . . Get up! Get up!— It's time to rush forward and throw grenades. It's time to take the trenches.—We're fighting with bayonets. We're in the German trenches. We're fighting with clubbed rifles and trench knives. There are screams and men running about in confusion. . . . Now everything is quiet again. We've started back with our prisoners.— Sergeant Dockdorf is lying with his throat cut, half in the trench and half out. . . . Jerry Easton is stretched on the German duckboards, his eyelids still fluttering. . . .

PRIVATE SAMUEL QUILLIN

IT was partly a dugout, and partly a dwelling, and it had been an officer's casino before we had taken the territory from the Germans, the day before. It faced the Somme-Py road, and immediately we turned it into an evacuation station. When I went up that night, to check the casualties in my battalion, the place was full of wounded men awaiting ambulances. It was in October, I remember, and the air was crisp, with a feeling of frost. For a few minutes I was busy going from man to man, looking at identification tags. Then I heard a whine and a rushing sound in the air. I covered my ears, and braced myself, because I knew by instinct that the shell was going to register a direct hit. The sound increased to a shriek. Then a flash of light and a thundering explosion that blew the walls outward, and I fell swiftly into a lake of ink and lay prone on the bottom and at peace, for a long time, not breathing . . . and then climbed out of the ink slowly, inch by inch, and began to groan. . . .

"There's a man alive down there," I heard somebody say. Nobody answered the voice for a moment. Then finally there came another voice: "Nobody could be alive with all that weight on him. . . ." Then I remembered where I was. I was lying on my back and through the beams, iron sheets and tons of earth, I could see one star, tired and faint in the sky. I became frightened and began to shout. . . .

"Lie quiet!" said the first voice sharply. "You've got to keep your head. . . . Lie quiet! and listen to what I say: There are hundreds of tons balanced over you. If you move about you'll bring it down." Then I became quiet. Above me I could see the men moving beams, but very cautiously, taking out the bodies as they came to them. The first man spoke to me again. "Are you hurt?" he asked.

"I suppose so," I said.

Then after a while I spoke again. "I'm going to start hollering: I'm thinking about those beams mashing me."

"You're a fool, if you do," he said.

I shut my eyes and began to compose a letter, in my mind, to a girl back home named Hazel Green, making each line rhyme. When I opened them, I could see a whole patch of sky. The patch got bigger and bigger until the last beam was lifted off my chest, and the men helped me out. I stood up, feeling my legs. I walked alone to the dressing station, and the doctor examined me, but there wasn't a scratch on me anywhere.

"Twenty-six men were taken out of that dugout, and you're the only one that came out alive," said the doctor. "You've had a lucky escape."

"Yes, sir, I sure did," I said.

PRIVATE ABRAHAM RICKEY

I WAS lying in the wheat near Captain Matlock when he got hit and I was the first man to reach him. One machine gun bullet had hit him squarely between the eyes, plowing through his head and coming out at the base of his skull.

A boy out of the third platoon, named Mart Passy, came up when I called, and together we lifted the Captain and carried him to a trench where stretcher bearers picked him up and took him to the rear.

After the fighting was over and we were back at Fly Farm getting a batch of replacements, I was telling some of the boys about how Fishmouth Terry got hit. "He fell down without making any noise," I said. "He just fell down in the wheat and doubled up. I thought he was dead, sure, but he was breathing all right when the stretcher bearers took him. It was just one bullet, but it went all the way through his head. When I turned him on his face, I saw a teaspoonful of brains had run out on the ground."

"Wait a minute now . . . take it easy, sailor!" said Sergeant Dunning. "How much brains did you say ran out of Fishmouth Terry's head? . . ."

"About a teaspoonful," I said.

Everybody shook their heads and shrugged their shoulders.

"Are you sure it was Captain Matlock you picked up?" the sergeant asked again.

"Why, yes," I said. "Sure it was."

Everybody began to laugh. . . . "Be reasonable!" said Vester Keith. "Be reasonable!—If that many brains ran out, it couldn't possibly have been *our* Terry!"

PRIVATE WILBUR BOWDEN

IT was pitch dark, not even a star shining, when I crawled into a deep shell hole, and lay there listening. I knew, at once, there was a wounded man with me in the shell hole: I don't know how I knew it: I couldn't see him, certainly, but I did know it. Then I drew my trench knife and braced myself, but he spoke to me in English. He was an outpost sentry from the First Battalion who had run into a German patrol, and been wounded. He whispered all this, his mouth close to my ear. The German trenches were only a short distance away, and we didn't dare make a sound that might be overheard.

"Where did they get you?" I whispered back.

He waited a long time to answer. "In the leg," he said.

I took off his first aid packet and straightened out the bandage as best I could. I didn't have a match, and I wouldn't have dared strike it, if I had. I unfastened his belt and pulled his breeches down. Then I slit his drawers with my knife.

"Which leg is it?" I asked.

"I'm not sure," he said slowly.

"I'll run my hand over your leg," I whispered, "and when I come to the wounded place, let me know, and I'll put on a bandage."

"All right," he said finally.

I ran my hand slowly down his left leg from thigh to knee, but he didn't flinch or give any sign of pain. Then I started on his right thigh, feeling cautiously. Suddenly he winced a little. "Is that the place?" I asked. . . . "Yes," he said.

His uniform was soaked with blood and my fingers were sticky from touching his legs. I put the bandage on the spot he had indicated and tied it tightly.

"Am I still bleeding?" he asked.

"No," I said, "you're not bleeding now." Then I added: "The wound must be pretty small, after all, because I couldn't even feel it."

"It's deep, I guess," he said.

When I got the bandage on, he said he felt sleepy, and would take a nap. "That's the ticket," I said. "You take a nap now, and as soon as I get back to the company, I'll send out a couple of stretcher bearers for you." He didn't answer me. He'd gone to sleep while I was talking to him.

When I got back to the line, an hour later, I told Sergeant Boss about the wounded man and he sent out for him, but the man was dead when they found him. We took him into the dugout, and looked at him by candle light: The first thing we saw was a wound in his side that you could lay your fist in. I stood there puzzled, while the men kidded me. Then I took off the bandage I had put on his leg: The skin was unbroken. In fact there wasn't a scratch on his whole body except the one place in his side, from which he had bled to death.

I've thought about that man a good many times, but I can't make heads or tails of it. Why did he flinch, and say he was wounded in the leg, when he wasn't? Did he really know where he was wounded? Or was it because he knew he was going to die, and my questions bothered him? Did he think it would be easier to let me have my way, and put on a bandage, since I insisted on it? I've thought it over a good many times, without coming to any conclusion.

PRIVATE EUGENE MERRIAM

I DELIVERED the message to Lieutenant Bartelstone and turned to go, but the Germans had started
shelling the wood again, and the Somme-Py road.

"You'd better wait until the barrage lifts," said Lieutenant Bartelstone.

"No, sir," I said; "I guess I'd better get on back to
Regimental.—I'll get through, all right."

"That's a pretty heavy barrage," he said; "you'd better wait awhile."

"I'll be-all right," I said; "I've been through a hundred worse than that. If I waited for every barrage to
lift, I wouldn't get many messages delivered."

"Yes, I guess that's right," said the lieutenant
laughing.

I turned up my coat collar, like it was a rain storm
I was going through, and began loping through the
woods. There were shells exploding in the tree-tops
and the wood was filled with red hot shrapnel. The
shrapnel swirled around and whimpered and sounded
like horses biting at each other's flanks. It was autumn
and the leaves of the trees were red and yellow and
brown. They kept raining down before my eyes like

dead birds falling to earth. The shelling seemed to get heavier, but I ran on and on. I knew it was useless to duck. . . . Then the woods opened and I saw the road.

"In just a minute now, I'll be out of the barrage and safe," I thought.

PRIVATE HERBERT MERRIAM

W HEN I got back from the hospital it was late
September and the Company was billeted in a
wood near Manorville. I asked Sergeant Boss about my
brother, Gene, our regimental runner.

"Well, no, I haven't seen him lately," he answered,
"but then we've been on the move most of the time
and I haven't seen anybody from Headquarters hardly."

"I'll go over to Regimental to-night and surprise
Gene," I said.

I threw my equipment down on an empty bunk but
Byron Long picked it up. "Why don't you take my
bunk, Herbie," he asked. "That one's broke.—You come
over here and swap with me."

"Well, for Christ sake!" I said laughing. "What's
come over you boys, anyway? Are you practicing up to
be boy scouts?"

Byron didn't say anything, but he looked away.

"I wouldn't go over to Regimental to see Gene," said
Sergeant Halligan.

"Why not?" I asked; "there aren't any regulations
against it, are there?"

"I just wouldn't go, that's all."

I stood there thinking for a minute; then my heart began to beat too fast. My knees seemed to get weak, and for a minute I thought I was going to fall down.

"Oh," I said . . . "Oh, I see!"

"Why don't you lie down on Byron's bunk for a while," said Frank Halligan. "It's over against the wall, out of the way, where nobody will be stepping over you. —Why don't you lie down and take a little nap? . . . You must be tired, after that trip from the hospital."

"All right," I said. "I think I will take a nap."

"Stretch out all the way," said Byron. "Here—I'll put my blankets over you, so you won't get cold."

Then each man thought up some reason for going outside. They went out, one by one, and stood in the cold until finally I was alone in the bunk house.

PRIVATE PETER STAFFORD

WHEN I came out from the ether, I didn't know, at first, where I was, but after a while my mind cleared up and I remembered I was in a hospital, and that they had just cut off my leg. Then the nurse gave me some medicine to swallow and the pain stopped. Everything seemed to get all mixed up. For a little while I would know where I was, and what had happened to me, and then I would doze off and think I was back home again.

I don't know what time it was when I heard people whispering above my bed. I opened my eyes and looked up and all I saw at first was an elderly lady, with a sweet face, looking down at me. For some reason I thought I was back in Little Rock and that the lady was one of our neighbors, a Mrs. Sellers, come to call on Mamma.

"Hello, Mrs. Sellers!" I said; "what in the world are you doing up here in *my* room?"

Then I seen the doctors and the nurse standing there beside the lady, and I knew where I was. The lady didn't say anything, but she smiled in a friendly way. When I seen my mistake, I spoke to the lady more politely. "I beg your pardon, ma'am," I said, "but at first I taken you for a lady who runs a boarding-house across the street from where I live."

The lady spoke in a very cultured voice: "Do I resemble her a great deal?"

"Yes, ma'am," I said; "you sure do!—Why if you had on a dust-apron and a boudoir cap, nobody could ever tell you two apart."

Then I knew by the look on the nurse's face that I had made a break. Later I learned that I had been addressing her Majesty, the Queen of England. When I discovered that, I asked the nurse to be sure and tell the queen that Mrs. Sellers was a respectable woman who enjoyed the good-opinion of everybody in Little Rock and she needn't feel ashamed of resembling her. The nurse said she and the queen were good friends and that she'd be sure and tell her the next time they had a visit together.

I never heard any more about it, but the mistake was unintentional on my part, and it was evidently regarded in that light by the queen. . . . I'll bet, though, she still remembers my error, and that she had had many a good laugh at my expense since that time.

PRIVATE SIDNEY BELMONT

THEY tell this story on the colonel of my regiment. He had come up to the line one afternoon, in a private's uniform, after having taken off his eagles, his belt and all other insignia of rank. While standing there inspecting the line, Gene Merriam came up with a message. When he saw the colonel, he stopped and saluted, in plain view. That made the colonel sore.

"Say, you stupid little so-and-so," he shouted, "haven't you got sense enough not to salute an officer on the line? Do you want every sniper in the German army to try to pick me off?" For a time he stood swearing and shaking his fist and then he began to feel sorry for Gene, who was blushing and looking down under the bawling out he was getting. . . .

"Listen," the colonel said, "in the future when you want to attract my attention on the line, don't salute me. Come up, instead, and kick me a couple of times and say: 'Listen to me, you dopey old son of a bitch!' That's the way to speak to me, when I'm on the line," said the colonel.

Later I heard that story told on the colonel of every regiment in France, but it really happened in my outfit.

PRIVATE RICHARD STARNES

AFTER the raid that night, we became confused, and unable to find the gap in our wire. There were five of us. Six, if you count the prisoner we had taken for questioning. While we stood there disputing, the Germans began throwing over gas shells. We took out our masks and put them on at once, but the prisoner didn't have a mask, and when the gas started choking him, he dropped down in terror and begged for his life. He cried and wrung his hands and talked about his mother and his home. We paid no attention to him. We wouldn't listen to what he was saying. Then he threw his arms around my knees and clung to me. I have never seen such cowardice. . . . I kept shoving him away with my foot, but he came back, time after time, crying and clinging to my legs. He was beginning to cough by that time, and water was coming out of his eyes.

Now here's the funny part of the story: As the little swine hugged my knees and cried, a curious feeling of pity came over me, and before I realized what I was doing, I had got down on my knees beside him. I put my arms around him. . . . "Take my mask, brother,"

I said gently.—I don't know why I did it. I've never been able to tell why I did it!—I must have been crazy. Certainly no man in his right mind would do a thing like that. . . .

If he'd had the slightest sense of decency, he'd have refused the mask, but he took it out of my hand and put it on. I hadn't really meant to give the mask to him. Why should I do a thing of that sort? . . . As soon as I realized what I'd done, I wanted to take the mask away from him, but I couldn't do that with the other men looking on.—You see what an impossible position I was in? . . .

"Yes," said the doctor, "I can see that."

"What right did he have to take the mask, when I didn't know what I was doing?—What right had he—"

"It was a fine thing to do," said the doctor.

"I tell you I was crazy," I shouted. "I was sorry the moment I had done it."

"Be quiet," said the doctor, "or you'll start bleeding again."

CORPORAL FREDERICK WILLCOXEN

IT was late October, the Germans were falling back all along the line, releasing towns which they had occupied for four years, and all day we saw French civilians, mostly old men and women, trudging to the rear, loaded down with their personal property. When we fell out for a ten-minute rest, we saw an old woman sitting against the side of a steep hill. Strapped to her back was a huge wicker basket filled with pots and pans and such things. Her face was wrinkled, and she seemed weak and all in. "Christ Almighty!" said Sergeant Halligan, "how can that poor old soul manage to lift such a load?"

"I don't know," I said, "but I'm going over and help her carry her stuff up the hill." I turned and walked toward her, and as I did so, she started shaking her fist at me. I stopped in surprise and spoke to her gently: "Don't be scared, Granny," I said; "I'm not going to hurt you." Then I smiled and walked toward her again, but she jumped up, at my approach, making a squeaking noise, and scurried up the side of the hill, basket and all, as quick as a lizard running up a wall. She went up so fast, I stood there with my mouth open.

When she got to the top, she spat at me and called me a pig.

Everybody laughed and tried to kid me. Mart Passy lay on the ground and roared. "Say, Fred," he called, "ask your girl friend to come down again and carry up the rolling kitchen for us."

SERGEANT MARVIN MOONEY

ONE day in the Argonne Forest we came on a wounded German soldier. It was early in the morning and frost had fallen the night before. The German lay huddled on his belly, and he must have been there all night, because when I turned him over, there was no frost on the place where he had been lying. His face was white and he was shivering. He wore eye-glasses with thick, dirty lenses.

When he saw me, he begged for a drink of water. I said: "It was different when you were raping Red Cross Nurses and cutting off the legs of children in Belgium, wasn't it? The shoe's on the other foot, now.— Here's some of your own medicine!" Then I straightened out his head with my foot and pounded his face with the butt of my rifle until it was like jelly. After that I opened my canteen and poured all the water I had on the ground, as I didn't want anybody to think it was giving him the water I minded. "Here's a drink of water for you," I said. . . .

If you think I'm lying, just ask Fred Terwilliger or Harry Althouse. They were with me at the time. . . . He was a crummy little fellow and his eye-glasses were tied around his ears with two pieces of common twine. His face was white and he kept shivering and rattling his teeth together. He was about five feet six, I should say, although he might have been an inch or so taller than that. Every time I hit him his knees jerked up a little.

PRIVATE OLIVER TECLAW

WE were going up to the front line one morning when somebody began calling my name excitedly. "Ollie," he shouted, "Ollie Teclaw!"

It was Sergeant Ernest, my old drill sergeant. He used to say I was the worst soldier he ever tried to train, in all of his years of service.

"Hello," I said.

"Say, did you ever learn to hold a bayonet proper?" he asked.

"Nope," I said; "never did."

"Did you get so you could qualify with a rifle?"

"Never could shoot a rifle, Sarge," I said; "never could do that."

We were getting farther apart and Sergeant Ernest cupped his mouth with his hands and began to shout: "How about grenades? Can you throw grenades?"

"No better than I could in training camp," I said.

Ernest shook his head and groaned. "For Christ sake! Hasn't nobody killed you yet?" he shouted.

"Uh-uh," I said. . . . "Not so far."

PRIVATE FRANKLIN GOOD

IT was November. The nights were cold and there was frost on the ground in the mornings. The roads were frozen, and hard as iron. The trees were all bare of leaves and their branches made a whispering sound in the wind like sandpaper. In the forest before us, the Germans were retreating steadily, their ammunition and equipment littering their trenches, their wounded abandoned on the ground. We came through the forest cautiously, watching out for mines.

We came on all that day, steadily. Then, toward dark, we saw the Meuse flowing before us. We hurried, at sight of the river, anxious to cross the bridge and dig in before night fell, but before we reached the bank, there came three explosions and the bridge flung upward before our eyes and slid into the swift current. We stood there looking at the wrecked bridge, blowing on our hands, our breath congealing into steam.

Then the engineers came up from the rear to construct a pontoon. We began digging in, by the bank, in anticipation of the barrage the Germans were certain to lay down on us. The engineers worked rapidly and the bridge was ready before the barrage began. But somebody had to swim the river and anchor the bridge to the opposite bank. Jerry Blandford volunteered to do this. He took off his clothes and plunged into the icy water, towing the frail pontoon behind him. When he reached the opposite bank, the barrage started. Then he tied the rope around a tree stump and the first man came over. The shells were striking all about us, throwing up spouts of water and clots of mud bigger than a man's body. Then, one by one, we ran quickly across the bridge and took up a position on the other side. At daybreak we were all over. Nine men had been killed crossing and the bridge partially destroyed and repaired three times. When the last man was over, the platoons were reorganized and the attack continued. We turned and looked back at the river and saw the engineers, as busy as ants, building another bridge which would be strong enough to bear the weight of our artillery.

THE UNKNOWN SOLDIER

WE were returning from a wiring party that quiet night and the men were in high spirits. Then two Maxims opened a deadly, enfilading fire, and one of my companions threw his hands up and fell without a sound. I stood there confused at the sudden attack, not knowing which way to turn. Then I heard some one shout: "Look out! Look out for the wire!" and I saw my companions, flat on their frightened bellies, scattering in all directions. I started to run, but at that moment something shoved me, and something took my breath away, and I toppled backward, and the wire caught me.

At first I did not realize that I was wounded. I lay there on the wire, breathing heavily. "I must keep perfectly calm," I thought. "If I move about, I'll entangle myself so badly that I'll never get out." Then a white flare went up and in the light that followed I saw my belly was ripped open and that my entrails hung down like a badly arranged bouquet of blue roses. The sight frightened me and I began to struggle, but the more I twisted about, the deeper the barbs sank in. Finally I could not move my legs any more and I knew, then, that I was going to die. So I lay stretched quietly, moaning and spitting blood.

I could not forget the faces of the men and the way they had scurried off when the machine guns opened up. I remembered a time when I was a little boy and had gone to visit my grandfather, who lived on a farm. Rabbits were eating his cabbages that year, so grandfather had closed all the entrances to his field except one, and he baited that one with lettuce leaves and young carrots. When the field was full of rabbits, the fun began. Grandfather opened the gate and let in the dog, and the hired man stood at the gap, a broomstick in his hand, breaking the necks of the rabbits as they leaped out. I had stood to one side, I remembered, pitying the rabbits and thinking how stupid they were to let themselves be caught in such an obvious trap.— And now as I lay on the wire, the scene came back to me vividly. . . . *I* had pitied the rabbits!—I, of all people . . .

I lay back, my eyes closed, thinking of that. Then I heard the mayor of our town making his annual address in the Soldiers' Cemetery at home. Fragments of his speech kept floating through my mind: "These men died gloriously on the Field of Honor! . . . Gave their lives gladly in a Noble Cause! . . . What a feeling of exaltation was theirs when Death kissed their mouths and closed their eyes for an Immortal Eternity! . . ."

Suddenly I saw myself, too, a boy in the crowd, my throat tight to keep back the tears, listening enraptured to the speech and believing every word of it; and at that instant I understood clearly why I now lay dying on the wire. . . .

The first shock had passed and my wounds began to pain me. I had seen other men die on the wire and I had said if it happened to me, I would make no sound, but after a while I couldn't stand the pain any longer and I began to make a shrill, wavering noise. I cried like that for a long time. I couldn't help it. . . .

Towards daybreak a German sentry crawled out from his post and came to where I lay. "Hush!" he said in a soft voice. "Hush, please!"

He sat on his haunches and stared at me, a compassionate look in his eyes. Then I began to talk to him: "It's all a lie that people tell each other, and nobody really believes," I said. . . . "And I'm a part of it, whether I want to be or not.—I'm more a part of it now than ever before: In a few years, when war is over, they'll move my body back home to the Soldiers' Cemetery, just as they moved the bodies of the soldiers killed before I was born. There will be a brass band and speech making and a beautiful marble shaft with my name chiseled on its base. . . . The mayor will be there also, pointing to my name with his thick, trembling forefinger and shouting meaningless words about glorious deaths and fields of honor. . . . And there will be other little boys in that crowd to listen and believe him, just as I listened and believed!"

"Hush," said the German softly. "Hush! . . . Hush!"

I began to twist about on the wire and to cry again. "I can't stand the thought of that! I can't stand it! . . . I never want to hear military music or high sounding words again: I want to be buried where nobody will ever find me.—I want to be wiped out completely . . ."

Then, suddenly, I became silent, for I had seen a way out. I took off my identification tags and threw them into the wire, as far as I could. I tore to pieces the letters and the photographs I carried and scattered the fragments. I threw my helmet away, so that no one could guess my identity from the serial number stamped on the sweatband. Then I lay back exultant!

The German had risen and stood looking at me, as if puzzled. . . . "I've beaten the orators and the wreath layers at their own game!" I said. . . . "I've beaten them all!—Nobody will ever use me as a symbol. Nobody will ever tell lies over my dead body now! . . ."

"Hush," said the German softly. "Hush! . . . Hush!"

Then my pain became so unbearable that I began to choke and bite at the wire with my teeth. The German came closer to me, touching my head with his hand. . . .

"Hush," he said. . . . "Hush, please. . . ."

But I could not stop. I thrashed about on the wire and cried in a shrill voice. The German took out his pistol and stood twisting it in his hand, not looking at me. Then he put his arm under my head, lifting me up, and kissed me softly on my cheek, repeating phrases which I could not understand. I saw, then, that he too, had been crying for a long time. . . .

"Do it quickly!" I said. "Quickly! . . . Quickly!"

He stood with trembling hands for a moment before he placed the barrel of his pistol against my temple, turned his head away, and fired. My eyes fluttered twice and then closed; my hands clutched and relaxed slowly.

"I have broken the chain," I whispered. "I have defeated the inherent stupidity of life."

"Hush," he said. "Hush! . . . Hush! . . . Hush! . . ."

PRIVATE CHARLES UPSON

THE first thing we noticed was the silence of the German artillery. Then our own artillery quit firing. We looked at each other, surprised at the sudden quietness and wondered what was the matter. A runner came up, out of breath, with a message from Divisional. Lieutenant Bartelstone, in command of our company, read it slowly and called his platoon sergeants together. "Pass word to the men to cease firing, the war is over," he said.

CORPORAL STEPHEN WALLER

COMPANY K went into action at 10:15 P.M. December 12th, 1917, at Verdun, France, and ceased fighting on the morning of November 11th, 1918, near Bourmont, having crossed the Meuse River the night before under shell fire; participating, during the period set out above, in the following major operations: Aisne, Aisne-Marne, St. Mihiel and Meuse-Argonne.

A number of men were cited for bravery, the following decorations having been actually awarded for meritorious service under fire: 10 Croix de Guerre (four of them with palms); 6 Distinguished Service Crosses; 2 Medals Militaire and 1 Congressional Medal of Honor, the latter being awarded to Private Harold Dresser, a man of amazing personal courage.

The percentage of casualties in killed, wounded in action, missing or evacuated to hospital suffering from disease, was considerably higher than average (332.8) percent.

Our commanding officer, Terence L. Matlock, Captain, was able and efficient and retained throughout the respect and the admiration to the men who served under him.

PRIVATE LEO BROGAN

THE Armistice had been signed, and for three days we had been moving across France, a short day's march behind the evacuating German army. It was raining: a thin, misty rain which fell straight down and penetrated to our shivering skin as we plowed raggedly down the muddy country roads. Seen through the slow rain, the country-side, with its barren brown fields and leafless woods, seemed very desolate, and the ruined villages were lonely against a sky as gray as pewter.

Occasionally we passed through a village which had been partially rebuilt, or only imperfectly destroyed, in which people still lived, and at such times the inhabitants stood in their doorways, silent, and a little frightened, and watched us go past; or occasionally we passed some splendid country estate which had, by its isolation, escaped any systematic shelling, and stood now, incongruously intact, beside the road, with its brick walls and its iron gates and its untrimmed hedges. It was near such a château that we received orders to fall-out for our noon meal. We drew to one side of the road and waited. Presently the company's rolling-kitchen, drawn by old Mamie the galley mule, lumbered up to the head of the column and pulled out from the road into an uncultivated field.

Hymie White of the Second Platoon slipped out of his pack and stretched his shoulders. When he had got the kinks out of his shoulders and had assembled his mess-gear, the kitchen had been set up and a circle had already formed around it. A boiler of steaming soup was being lifted to the ground by Sidney Borgstead and his assistant cook. Sergeant Mike Olmstead, the company mess-sergeant, who was loudly supervising the preparations for the meal, turned suddenly, and spoke to us: "What are you birds trying to pull off? You get in line, or you don't get no chow, see?" Long association with hungry men had made Mike suspicious of everything. Mike had a lumpy, badly molded face, and a ragged mouth which resembled a small shell hole.

A line quickly formed and Sid Borgstead commenced dishing out the food. Sergeant Olmstead stood by to see that each man got his fair share. When Hymie White's turn came, he was served with a dipper full of thin soup and a small slice of bread over which a spoonful of corn syrup had been poured. He looked at the scant rations and was furious all of a sudden.

"That's a hell of a meal to offer a man!" he said. The friendly look was gone from his eyes; his face was flushed and his nostrils dilated. "That's a fine God damned meal to offer a man!"

"If you don't like it, put it back in the pot," said Sergeant Olmstead.

"I haven't had enough to eat since I joined this bastardly outfit!"

"Don't tell me your troubles, sonny!"

"What this company needs most is a new mess-sergeant!"

"Yeah?" said Sergeant Olmstead. "Well, let me tell you something. I cook what Headquarters issues me, see?"

It was then that Hymie realized the futility of further argument. He walked back to the roadside where he had left his pack and sat down upon it to eat his meal. He noticed that several very old men and very young children had, in his absence, gathered by the iron gate of the château. They gazed steadily at the soldiers eating their food, following with slow eyes the rhythmic rise and fall of a hundred dirty spoons.

Presently an old lady, wrapped in a waterproof coat, came hobbling down the long, flag-paved walk that ran from the iron gate to the château. With her was a girl about eight years old: a homely child with tight pig-tails and bangs and fat, clumsy legs. Beside the child there walked, sedately, a young fawn, with dappled gray sides and soft brown eyes.

When the party reached the gate the old lady dramatically placed one bony hand upon her heart and

with a wide, inclusive gesture she blew a kiss to the re-
clining soldiers. Then she began to speak rapidly in
French, clutching her heart, or her throat, at intervals,
and at intervals pointing to the dull sky. Hymie turned
and spoke to Pierre Brockett: "What the hell is the old
bag making a speech about?" Brockett, who had been
sopping his pan with a morsel of bread to get the last
drop of soup, looked up and listened for a moment:
"She's thanking the brave soldiers for saving her stricken
France, and so on, and so on." "Oh, is that what it's all
about?" said Hymie.

Then he noticed that the fawn had thrust its head
between the iron bars of the gate and was regarding
him, across the muddy road, with eager, infatuated eyes.
Hymie whistled softly—ingratiatingly. Instantly the little fawn lunged against the gate, a ripple of excitement
passing over its nervous body. It stood there trembling
for a moment, then it withdrew from the gate and
minced across the lawn, switching its fluff of a tail and
running in sudden, clowning circles. Finally it stopped
and looked at Hyman White to see if its efforts had been
appreciated.

The soldiers laughed loudly at its antics. At the
sound of their laughter the old lady paused in her
speech, her right hand pointing straight up to the spot
in the sky that she considered the abode of God, and
the other resting on the black head of the little girl, who

had turned and was clapping her hands in delight. The old lady smiled indulgently, stroked the cheek of the little girl, and, with another blown kiss and a low bow, brought to an end her speech. A dozen soldiers crowded in front of the gate, snapping their fingers and whistling to attract the attention of the fawn, but it ignored them: it gazed with fascinated eyes at Hyman White, alone.

"Try it again, Hymie!" said Graley Borden.

Again Hymie gave his long, soft whistle and, as if awaiting that signal, the little fawn ran crazily up the walk, kicking its heels in the air and showing the creamy softness of its belly. It made sudden, idiotic rushes at flower-beds and leafless shrubs, bracing itself quickly in time to avoid a collision, only to dash off, crazily, at another angle. At length it ran toward the iron gate and again hurled itself against the bars. Unable to escape as it wished, it stood looking at the old lady, its dappled hide twitching with nervous excitement.

The men who had gathered in front of the gate were delighted with the diversion. They laughed loudly and made ribald remarks about the power of love at first sight and Hyman White's unsuspected prowess as a charmer. There was a tender smile on the old lady's face, and suddenly she unfastened the great catch on the iron gate. There came a sharp cry and a quick sentence from the little girl, but the old lady patted her cheek and spoke a dozen soft, reassuring words in reply.

For a moment there was silence, then the little girl nodded her head and stood stolidly regarding her boots. At the child's nod, the old lady swung wide the gate and the little fawn instantly leaped out and ran across the muddy road, hurling itself into the arms of Hyman White.

The soldiers crowded around him, trying to attract the fawn's attention, but it would not notice them: It would not move from the arms of Hyman White where it lay licking his cheek with its soft tongue, and gazing at him with loving, humid eyes.

I stood with John McGill watching the picture. John was considerably affected. He turned to me and spoke softly: "How surer than our human reason is the simple instinct of the fawn. . . . There must be a beauty of soul in Hyman White, instantly apparent and compelling to the fawn, that escapes our duller senses."

I looked at Hymie White for a minute and saw a stocky, stolid lad, with heavy features and reddened face. His mouth was stained with grease from the soup which he had just eaten, and his nose dripped a little.

"Maybe so, John," I said. "Maybe so."

After a while word came down the line for us to stand by. We rose and collected our packs and our scattered mess-gear.

Hyman White was still holding the little fawn in his arms, passing his hands lovingly over its soft, fat flanks.

Finally he turned to Pierre Brockett, who was struggling into his marching-order.

"Ask the old girl what she'll take for the fawn," he said.

Brockett stated the question and again there came a quick, terrified cry from the little girl, but the old lady smiled and shook her head.

"Won't sell it," said Pierre.

Hymie walked regretfully across the road and put down the fawn beside the little girl. The fawn struggled and tried to free itself, but the little girl held it tightly in her arms. When Hymie had reached his place, and had thrown his rifle across his shoulder, the little girl burst into tears and spoke rapidly to the old lady. A moment later she released the fawn and it ran quickly to Hymie, again nuzzling his hand, and dancing around him.

The old lady held up her arm for attention. The troops turned to regard her. She spoke rapidly for a few moments, and Brockett translated to the troops, who were already moving off. "She says that she would never sell the fawn—no, no! not for any amount of money! But since the brave soldier and the fawn love each other so dearly, her granddaughter gives it to him gladly!"

The little girl took a step forward and spoke in a shrill treble. Then she stopped quickly, as if reproved, and looked at the muddy earth.

"Take care of him! Take care of him!" said Pierre Brockett. Then he added: "She says the fawn is very gentle."

Hymie looked back for an instant and waved his hand to the old lady, and the little girl, but the old lady did not see him; she had commenced speaking again, with sweeping gestures that included, impartially, the soldiers, the rain soaked country-side and the dull sky. There were still tears in the eyes of the little girl, and she gazed longingly at the fawn. In her heart there was a hope that the fawn, at last, would come to its senses and return to her, but the fascinated creature skipped up and down the side of the muddy road, and did not once look back.

The thin rain continued to fall. We walked in silence except for the occasional tinkle of a canteen and the monotonous sucking sound of many feet sinking and being withdrawn from the soft mud. Gradually the dark set in. Then Hymie lifted the fawn into his arms where it lay with its muzzle resting in the harness of his pack. When it was almost dark we reached the town where we were to sleep for the night. Roy Winters, our billeting sergeant, who had gone on before us, was waiting, and directed the company to its assigned space. When Hymie had got his squad all settled and had laid out his pack on the dry straw, he whistled to his fawn and went outside. I got up and followed him, and in the road in front of the billet, he spoke to me:

"Where has Mike set up his galley?" he asked.

"I don't know," I said.

He turned away and walked off, but I followed him at a short distance, dodging out of sight when he turned his head.

He found Mike, in an old stable, his kitchen set up and a great fire roaring. Sidney Borgstead was peeling potatoes and dropping them into a dirty, smoke-encrusted bucket at his side.

Hymie and the fawn entered the stable and I stood by the door, peering in, and listening to what they said.

"Get out of here!" said Sergeant Olmstead irritably; "supper ain't ready for an hour yet."

"Sergeant," said Hymie in a wheedling, placating voice, "I've got a proposition for you—just you and me."

"Yeah? What is it?" replied Mike, still suspicious.

Hymie hesitated for a moment, somewhat embarrassed. The dappled fawn was exploring the dark recesses of the stable, stepping daintily back and forth in the red light from the fire, and pretending to be frightened at a brown leaf blowing slowly across the unever floor.

"Did you ever eat venison steaks?" he asked at last.

Mike's ragged, slack mouth opened a little in sur-

prise. "Hell, man— You don't mean you're going to—!"
. . . He paused, slightly shocked at the idea.

"I'm hungry," said Hymie. Then he added: "It'll be just me and you, sergeant; what do you say?"

"But say, you couldn't do that; not after the way the fawn took to you, and all. . . . ."

"Sure I could. Why not?"

Mike rubbed his lumpy nose for a time. Finally he said: "A stew would be better—a stew with onions and potatoes in it."

"That's up to you, Mike; whatever you say is all right with me."

Then Mike laughed, as if ashamed, and nodded his head.

At Hymie's whistle the fawn turned quickly, and faced him. . . . The firelight gilded the soft cream of its throat and turned to dark copper the gray markings on its flanks. Its sweet brown eyes were bright with love as it ran quickly to Hymie White, and rubbed its nose against his knee, dancing about him.

"Pass me that breadknife!" said Hymie to Mike Olmstead.

PRIVATE ROBERT ARMSTRONG

THE curtains parted and a secretary in a tailor-made uniform came onto the stage. Behind him we could see the orchestra, seated in a semi-circle, tuning their instruments. The secretary bowed to us and smiled. "Oh, I know soldiers hate speech making," he said, "but I have been delegated to make you an address of welcome, so I suppose I must go ahead and do my *darnedest!*" He laughed delicately and the men, after looking at each other, laughed too. There was an irregular clapping of hands. When it died, the secretary continued.

"I'm sure you will agree that this is the strangest dance you ever attended. At first we wondered how to give a dance at all without members of the fair sex present. Some of the organization were in favor of inviting local girls, but I'm glad to say that idea was overruled: We felt that was not fair to you fine young men." The secretary's voice became grave. "I'm sure you know what I mean . . . fellows!" There was silence for a moment, and then the secretary shook his head a couple of times and went on.

"Finally somebody had a happy thought and suggested that we invite boys from the various church homes and dress them up in women's costumes, thus preserving the element of exercise, and at the same time eliminating the more objectionable features of the dance."

The men looked at each other sheepishly. A few of us began to move toward the door, but the secretary stopped us. "But wait!" he said, holding up his hand for silence. "We have *another* surprise for you!—Two of the 'girls' present will really *be* girls! They have come all the way from the canteen in Coblenz, and their presence lends an added charm to the occasion."

Again the secretary smiled and showed his gleaming teeth. Then the folding doors to the right opened and the female impersonators entered. They were dressed in a variety of fancy costumes, but Pierretes and Highland Lassies predominated. They stood in the center of the room and stared at the soldiers who lined the walls, and who, in turn, stared at them.

The secretary came back upon the stage and clapped his hands. "Fellows!—Fellows! Get into the spirit of the occasion, please!—No introductions are necessary, I assure you!"

Coming back that night Jim Dunning spoke suddenly, as if something had just occurred to him. "Say, did any of you guys run across the canteen dames the secretary mentioned?"

Frank Halligan spoke up. "I didn't dance with them, but they were those two who sat over by the palms all evening."

"Is that who they were?" asked Jim in surprise. "Well, that's rich; that sure is a good one on me.—I thought those two were a couple of mule skinners from Headquarters company!"

PRIVATE CHRISTIAN VAN OSTEN

IT was the Fourth of July following the Armistice, and early that morning Mrs. Steiner called at the hospital. She and her husband were in Paris buying for their chain of department stores and they wanted to entertain three American soldiers in honor of the day. . . . "We want you to send soldiers wounded in action," she kept repeating to the head nurse, "but nothing gruesome, you understand: nothing really revolting or gruesome! . . ." So the nurse selected a fellow from the First Engineers called "Bunny," a man from the Rainbow Division named Towner, and myself.

We were ready when the automobile came by for us, and a little later we were in Mr. Steiner's suite at the Ritz. He was a nervous, bald-headed little man and he kept hopping about like a bird. "We were afraid you boys might be timid about ordering expensive dishes, and try to let us off too easy, so dinner has already been ordered," he said. Nobody answered, so Mr. Steiner continued, rubbing his hands together. "Soak me good, boys!—I may not be the richest man in the United States, but I can stand a little gouging, I guess!"

"Adolph!" said Mrs. Steiner laughing and shaking her

head; "Adolph! Don't be always talking about money."

"Well, it's true, ain't it?" asked Mr. Steiner. "I'm a rich man; why should I try to hide it?"

A little later two waiters brought up the dinner and began to serve it. "Lift up your plates," said Mr. Steiner, "and see what Santa Claus put in your stocking."

There was a fifty dollar bill under each plate. "Oh, say, now," said Bunny. "I can't really take this! . . ." "Take it and put it in your pocket quick," said Mrs. Steiner, winking; "there's plenty more where that came from!"

The dinner was excellent, and as each course was served Mr. Steiner told us what that individual item had cost him. "I don't begrudge it, though," he repeated; "I want you boys to have the very best of everything to-day. You've been through hell for us folks back home, and I say there's nothing too good for you now!"

At last dinner was over and we were having liquers. "How about a cigar?" asked Mr. Steiner. Bunny and I said we'd rather smoke a cigarette, but Towner accepted. Mr. Steiner called the waiter and told him to go to the adjoining room and fetch the box of cigars he would find on the writing desk. The waiter did so, and a moment later he was offering the box to Towner. Towner took one, and was just about to bite off the end, when Mr. Steiner stopped him excitedly. "No!—

No!" he shouted angrily at the waiter.—"That's the wrong box!" Towner returned the cigar and Mr. Steiner came over and took the box from the waiter. "Get the other box," he said; "the one on the writing desk, like I told you!"

Then he turned to Towner, tapping the box against his palm. "These cigars are made especially for me," he said in explanation. "You can't buy them in a shop."

"Adolph!" said Mrs. Steiner quickly. "Why, Adolph!"

Mr. Steiner began to look ashamed. "It's not the fact that those cigars retail for a dollar and fifty cents each," he said apologetically; "that's got nothing to do with it at all. But you see I've got so I can't smoke anything else, and I only got three boxes left to last me until I get back to the States. . . ." He put his hand on Towner's shoulder. "You understand my position in the matter, don't you?"

Towner said sure, he understood perfectly, and that he'd just as soon have a cigar out of the other box. He said it didn't make a particle of difference to him one way or the other.

PRIVATE ALBERT HAYES

IN addition to the chocolate and cigarettes which were sold to us at three times their regular value, the canteen put in a line of sweaters and knitted socks. It was cold in the trenches and I wanted one of the sweaters to wear next to my skin to keep me warm at nights. I picked out a yellow one because it looked comfortable, and paid the canteen ten dollars for it. After I got back to my billet, and was examining it closely, I discovered there was a tiny pocket knitted in the bottom of the sweater and that a piece of paper had been tucked into it. Here's what I read:

"I am a poor old woman, seventy-two years old, who lives at the poor farm, but I want to do something for the soldier boys, like everybody else, so I made this sweater and I am turning it over to the Ladies Aid to be sent to some soldier who takes cold easy. Please excuse bad knitting and bad writing. If you get a cold on your chest take a dose of cooking soda and rub it with mutton suet and turpentine mixed and don't get your feet wet if you can help it. I used to be a great hand to knit but now I am almost blind. I hope a poor boy gets this sweater. It's not a very good one but I have put my love in every stitch and that's something that can't be bought or sold.

"Your obedient servant,

"(Mrs.) MARY L. SAMFORD.

"P.S. Don't forget to say your prayers at night and please write regularly to your dear mother."

PRIVATE ANDREW LURTON

THEY saw from my service record book that I had been a court reporter on the outside, so they ordered me up to Regimental where Lieutenant Fairbrother, acting as Judge Advocate, was prosecuting General Courts.

On Monday a kid from my company named Ben Hunzinger got fifteen years hard labor for deserting in the face of the enemy, and a long talk from Mr. Fairbrother about justice tempered with mercy. On Tuesday a man from the First Battalion was awarded five years for leaving his post, thirty kilometers behind the lines, in order to warm his feet in the bunk house. On Wednesday it was a man named Pinckney who had gone nuts, after Soissons, and shot himself in the foot. He got eight and one-half years. . . . Why exactly eight years and six months?—I've never been able to figure that out. . . .

Then, on Thursday and Friday we had a big, front-page case. A sergeant named Vindt and a private named Neidlinger were accused of certain acts together and were sentenced, on the unsupported word of a sergeant, getting the limit that the court martial manual permitted. Fairbrother made another long speech—that lad will speak at the drop of a hat—about how Vindt and Neidlinger were blots on American citizenship, the flag, the home, etc., etc. He regretted he could not, by law, order them shot like dogs. I took it all down. . . . "I had no idea that such things actually existed!" he kept repeating in his fine, mellow voice. . . . (Well, you'd better go see your old nursie when you get home and ask her a few questions, I thought.)

But the funniest case of all was reserved for Saturday. The man on trial was named Louis de Lessio. He had been sent back to an officers' training school, in the rear, but he hadn't got his bars, and for some reason or other he was returned to the company. Sergeant Donohoe, it seemed, had ordered him to go on a working party to repair roads, and reported later to Captain Matlock that de Lessio had refused to go, saying: "To hell with you and Fishmouth Terry!—I don't intend soldiering until they send me my commission."

De Lessio denied saying this. He stated that what he had really said was: "Very well, Sergeant Donohoe; I shall be extremely glad to go on your working party, because I realize that I shall have to soldier harder than ever now, if I expect to receive my commission. . . ." Sergeant Donohoe had thirty-two witnesses to prove his story, but de Lessio found thirty-five men who had understood him to say what he claimed. It went back and forth that way all day, and half the night.

I wish the lads who talk about the nobility and comradeship of war could listen to a few general courts. They'd soon change their minds, for war is as mean as poor-farm soup and as petty as an old maid's gossip.

PRIVATE HOWARD BARTOW

AFTER that first trip to the trenches, I made up my mind that I would not go back again. Of course I had no idea of deserting like Chris Geils or Ben Hunzinger: That, obviously, was as stupid as going to the line and getting shot. I determined to keep my eyes open and use my head.

I knew, in May, from what the French told us, that something was coming off, so when an order came around asking for one man from each company to attend grenade school, I put in for the place. There were no other applicants. As our company went to the front in crowded camions, I passed to the rear seated comfortably in a truck. When I rejoined my company, the fighting at Belleau Wood was over, and the handful of men who had survived were behind the lines again.

Then, in July, any idiot could have seen the obvious preparations for another drive. So I managed, while on a working party, to let one end of the field desk fall on my foot. The three weeks in the hospital that followed were really delightful, and when I got back, Soissons was a thing of the past. It amused me to hear that that ass, Matlock, had instructed Steve Waller, his clerk, to prepare court martials for several men, because of self-inflicted wounds. Waller didn't quite know how to do it, so I helped him with his forms, making them all air-tight. It was most amusing.

In September I went back to Divisional Headquarters as an interpreter. They soon found out that my French was the elementary French of a school-boy, and that I knew no word of German. But I was so contrite and so anxious to please, that the staff officers hated to return me to my company. "You've seen a lot of service," they said; "and a little rest won't do you any harm. You'd better stick around for a few days, anyway, and join your company when it comes out. . . ."

I thought, though, they had me in November, when we were entering the Argonne, but I volunteered to take a message back to Regimental Headquarters. On my way to the rear, I decided to take a chance. I lay hidden in a cellar in Les Eyelettes for six days, and when I joined my company at Pouilly, the day after the Armistice was signed, I told a story of having been captured by Germans. Nobody doubted the story, because I was careful to make my part in it unheroic and ridiculous.

During my entire enlistment I was in only one barrage. I never fired my rifle a single time. I never even saw a German soldier except a few prisoners at Brest, in a detention camp. But when we paraded in New York, nobody knew I had not been through as much as any man in the company. Just as many silly old women cried over me and I had just as many roses thrown at my head as were thrown at the heads of Harold Dresser, Mart Passy or Jack Howie. You've got to use your brains in the army, if you expect to survive!

PRIVATE WILLIAM NUGENT

THE warden asked me again if I wouldn't see the chaplain. "What the hell do I want to see him for?" I asked. "Say, listen to me—you'd better keep that bird out of here, if you don't want to get him told! If there's anything I hate worse than cops, it's preachers!" I said.

Everybody in the House was listening to me telling the warden. "I'm a tough baby," I said. "I bumped that cop off. Sure I did. I never denied that at the trial, did I? . . . It wasn't the first one, either. I'd bump off a dozen more, right now, if I had a chance. . . . Tell the chaplain that for me, will you? . . ."

Then the warden went away and after a while my cell door opened and the chaplain come in. He had a Bible in his hand with a purple ribbon to mark the place. He come in softly and closed the door behind him, a couple of guards standing outside to see I didn't harm him none.

"Repent, my son, and give your soul to God! Repent and be saved before it is too late!"

"Get out of here!" I said. "Get out! I don't want to have nothing to do with you!"

"You have sinned, my son," he said. "You have sinned

in the sight of Almighty God. . . . 'Thou shalt not kill!'—Those are the words of our blessed Lord. . . ."

"Listen," I said. "Don't pull that stuff on me, or I'll laugh in your face. I'm wise to how things are done. . . . Sure I killed that cop," I said. "I hate cops! Something burns me up and I get dizzy every time I see one. I bumped that cop, all right. Why not? . . . Who the hell are cops to make a man do things he don't want to do? . . . Say, let me tell you something about a big job I pulled once when I was in the army. I was a young fellow then, and I believed all the boloney you're talking now. I believed all that. . . . Well, anyway, we took a bunch of prisoners one day. It was too much trouble to send 'em back to the rear, so the cop of my outfit made us take 'em into a ditch, line 'em up and shoot 'em. Then, a week later when we were back in rest billets, he lined the company up and made us all go to church to listen to a bird like you talk baloney. . . ."

"My son," said the chaplain, "this is the last day of your life. Can't you realize that? Won't you let me help you? . . ."

"Get out of here," I said, and began to curse the chaplain with every word I knew. "You get out of here! If there's anything I hate worse than cops, it's preachers! . . . You get out!"

The preacher closed his Bible, and the guards opened

the door. "I guess I got that bastard told!" I said; "I guess I blew his ears down for him!"

The other boys in the House began to beat on the sides of their cells. "That's telling him, kid!" they said; "that's telling him!" Then I sat down on the side of my bunk and waited for them to come in and slit my pants and shave my head.

PRIVATE RALPH NERION

WHY didn't they make me a non-commissioned officer? I knew the I.D.R. backwards and forwards. I'm intelligent, and I have natural executive ability: I could command a squad, a platoon, or a company, for that matter. Did you ever stop to think about that? Do you realize I participated in all the action my company saw? I was with Wilbur Tietjen and Mart Passy on most of their exploits. They received fame and decorations and French generals kissed them and commended them before the Regiment. But did I get any recognition for what I did? Ha, ha, ha! Please don't be ridiculous! . . .

They had it in for me from the very beginning: Sergeant Olmstead instructed his cooks to give me the worst ration of beef and the smallest and dirtiest of the potatoes. Even the supply sergeant had it in for me: When he got in new shoes, or new uniforms, he could never find the sizes I wore. Oh, no! Not *my* size: but he could find the *same* sizes for Archie Lemon or Wilbur Halsey! . . . So I went into the service a private and came out a private. I went in unknown and was discharged the same way, without recognition. I know why, of course: in fact I didn't expect anything else. . . .

Those remarks I made about the United States Government and President Wilson were overheard and repeated in Washington, and secret service men have trailed me ever since. Do they think I did not know that Pig Iron Riggin is in the secret service? Or that he watched me like a hawk, hoping that I would betray myself? . . . I didn't mind it in the army, so much, but now that war is over why can't they let me alone? Why don't they stop following me home and calling me on the telephone, only to hang up when I have answered? Why do they write letters to my employer, trying to get me discharged? Who is that mysterious person my wife talks to down the air-shaft? . . . I tell you I can't stand this continual persecution much longer. . . .

PRIVATE PAUL WAITE

I ENLISTED the day after war was declared, but my brother, Rodger, sat around talking about the barbarity of the Germans, selling Liberty Bonds and making speeches. Then, finally, the draft got him and he came to France, just in time to get into action for two days in the Argonne before the Armistice was signed. (I'd been in the service a year and a half by that time, and on the line constantly for almost eight months.)

On the last day of the fighting Rodger got his shoulder nicked by a piece of shrapnel, or at least that's what he said; anyway, it was so small you couldn't even see the scar when I got back home, almost a year later. So Rodger was sent to a hospital and returned to the United States. They made a hell of a lot over him when he got home, the first of the returning soldiers, and all that sort of thing. He sat in an arm chair on the front porch impersonating a wounded war hero, talking to old ladies and admiring young girls.

It was pretty soft for Rodger, but when I got home everybody was sick of the war. "Now, dear," said my mother, "Rodger has told us all about it. I know it must be painful to think about those things, so you don't have to talk about them. Rodger has told us everything. . . ."

"Is that so?" I asked. "Well, I wonder who told Rodger about it?"

"Now, Paul," said my mother, "you're not being fair to your brother."

But I wanted to talk anyhow. At the supper table that night I was telling about a gas attack, when Rodger stopped me. "No," he said, "that wasn't the way it was done." Then I spoke of airplanes coming down close to the road and spraying troops with machine guns.

"That's really absurd," said Rodger; "I never saw anything like that when I was in France."

"How the hell could you," I said. "Your excursion ticket was only good for three days. How could you see anything in that time! . . ."

Rodger turned his head away and lay back in his chair. "Please . . ." he said in a gasping voice. Then Mamma ran over and put her arms around him, and my sisters looked at me angrily. "I guess you're satisfied, now that you've made poor Rodger sick again!" they said.

I turned and walked to my room. A little later my mother stood in the door. "You shouldn't treat your brother so unsympathetically," she said. "After all, Rodger *was* wounded, dear!"

SERGEANT JACK HOWIE

THE people in Savannah treated us fine. They gave us a party that night and all the girls in town were there to dance with us. One of them took a shine to me right off the reel. She was the prettiest girl at the party, too. She had dark eyes, and dark curly hair, and her skin was as white as milk. On her left cheek, almost up to her eyebrows, were three brown moles that formed a triangle. The one at the top was a little larger than the other two, but not much. When she saw me she came straight past all the other men, and asked me to dance with her. Gee! I thought I'd fall over backwards.

When I had her in my arms I kept thinking: "Good Lord! If I gave you a good squeeze you'd break right in two! . . ." I kept stepping on her feet and bumping into her knees, but this little girl said I danced fine. My hands felt as big as skinned pork loins and my uniform seemed too tight for me. Then we went outside and sat in the moonlight. Say, this was the most beautiful girl I ever saw. I thought her eyes were brown at first, but they weren't brown at all: they were dark blue. Her hair smelled like violets. I wanted to put my arms around her, but I didn't dare make a break. I kept thinking: "Gee, what a help you'd be to a man on a farm! . . ."

I don't like to tell this part of it, but after a while she said: "You are the handsomest man I have ever seen." I giggled like a fool. "Say, what are you trying to hand me, sister?" I asked. Then I wanted to kick myself for saying that. "I sounded just like a village yokel that time!" I thought. . . .

But the little girl didn't seem to hear me. She touched my cheek with her fingers. "Will you be my perfect knight, without fear and without reproach? . . ." I didn't say anything, but this thought crossed my mind: "She's talking like that because I've got on a uniform. If she'd seen me first in dirty overalls working on a farm, she wouldn't so much as speak to me." I turned away from her and sat up straight. . . . "The fine lady of the castle sending one of the peasant boys off to war!" I thought. . . . Then I stood up and yawned. "Don't talk silly," I said. . . .

But this little girl I'm telling you about got up too. She put her arms around my neck and kissed me on the mouth. "Never forget me!" she whispered; "never forget me as long as you live!" I took her arms away and began to laugh. "Don't be a fool," I said; "I won't even remember you to-morrow! . . ."

But all during war times I thought about her, and I pictured, a thousand times, my return to Savannah to show her my medal, and to tell her that I'd been her knight as well as I knew how, not talking dirty or having anything to do with street walkers, or anything like that. But when war was really over I went straight back home and took over the farm. (A swell help *she'd* have been to a man on a farm!) Then I got to going with Lois Shelling and we married soon after that. Lois and me get along fine together. So the girl in Savannah was wrong about my not forgetting her: I can't even remember now what she looked like.

PRIVATE ARTHUR CRENSHAW

WHEN I came home the people in my town declared "Crenshaw Day." They decorated the stores and the streets with bunting and flags; there was a parade in the morning with speeches afterwards, and a barbecue at Oak Grove in the afternoon.

Ralph R. Hawley, President of the First National Bank and Trust Company, acted as toastmaster. He recited my war record and everybody cheered. Then he pointed to my twisted back and my scarred face and his voice broke with emotion. I sat there amused and uncomfortable. I wasn't fooled in the slightest. There is an expressive vulgar phrase which soldiers use on such occasions and I repeated it under my breath.

At last the ceremonies were over and Mayor Couzens, himself, drove me in his new automobile to my father's farm beyond the town. The place had gone to ruin in my absence. We Crenshaws are a shiftless lot, and the town knows it. The floors were filthy, and there was a pile of unwashed dishes in the sink, while my sister Maude sat on the step eating an apple, and gazing, half asleep, at a bank of clouds. I began to wonder what I could do for a living, now that heavy farm work was impossible for me any more. All that afternoon I thought and at last I hit on the idea of starting a chicken farm. I got pencil and paper and figured the thing out. I decided that I could start in a small way if I had five hundred dollars with which to buy the necessary stock and equipment.

That night as I lay awake and wondered how I could raise the money, I thought of Mr. Hawley's speech in which he had declared that the town owed me a debt of gratitude for the things I had done which it could never hope to repay. So the next morning I called on him at his bank and told him of my plans, and asked him to lend me the money. He was very courteous and pleasant about it; but if you think he lent me the five hundred dollars you are as big a fool as I was.

PRIVATE EVERETT QUALLS

ONE by one my cattle got sick and fell down, a bloody foam dripping from their jaws and nostrils. The veterinarians scratched their heads and said they had never seen anything like it. I knew what was the matter, but I didn't say anything, and at last my stock was all dead. I breathed with relief then. "I have paid for what I did," I thought; "now I can start all over." But about that time a blight came upon my corn, which was well up and beginning to tassel: the joints secreted a fluid which turned red over night. The green blades fell off and the stalks withered and bent to the ground. . . . "This, too!" I thought; "this, too, is required of me!"

My crops were ruined, my cattle dead. I talked it over with my young wife. She kissed me and begged me not to worry so. "We can live some way this winter," she said. "We'll start again in the Spring. Everything will be all right."

I wanted to tell her then, but I didn't dare do it. I couldn't tell her a thing of that sort. And so I went about hoping that He had forgotten and that my punishment was lifted. Then my baby, who had been so strong and healthy, took sick. I saw him wasting away before my eyes, his legs and arms turning purple, his eyes glazed and dead with the fever, his breathing sharp and strained.

I had not prayed for a long time, but I prayed now. "Oh, God, don't do this," I pleaded. "It's not his fault; it's not the baby's fault. I, I alone am guilty. Punish me, if You will—but not this way! . . . Not this way, God! . . . Please! . . ." I could hear my baby's breath rattling in the next room; I could hear the hum of the doctor's voice, the clink of an instrument against glass and the worried words of my wife. Then the baby's breathing stopped altogether and there was my wife's intaken wail of despair.

I beat my breast and flung myself to the floor and that scene I had tried to crush from my mind came back again. I could hear Sergeant Pelton giving the signal to fire and I could see those prisoners falling and rising and falling again. Blood poured from their wounds and they twisted on the ground, as I was twisting now on the floor. . . . One of the prisoners had a brown beard and clear, sunburned skin. I recognized him to be a farmer, like myself, and as I stood above him, I imagined his life. He, too, had a wife that he loved who waited for him somewhere. He had a comfortable farm and on holidays, at home, he used to drink beer and dance. . . .

My wife was knocking on the door, but I would not

let her in. Then I knew what I must do. I took my service revolver, climbed out of my window and ran to the grove of scrub oaks that divided my land. When I reached the grove, I put the barrel in my mouth and pulled the trigger twice. There came blinding pain and waves of light that washed outward, in a golden flood, and widened to infinity. . . . I lifted from the ground and lurched forward, feet first, borne on the golden light, rocking gently from side to side. Then wild buffaloes rushed past me on thundering hooves, and receded, and I toppled suddenly into blackness without dimension and without sound.

PRIVATE HAROLD DRESSER

THE French Government gave me a Croix de Guerre with palm for crawling out in a barrage and rescuing a wounded French captain and his orderly. That was in April, 1918. Then, in July, I destroyed, single handed, a machine gun nest that was holding up our advance and killing many of our men, and I got both the Medal Militaire and the D.S.C. for that. I got the Medal of Honor in October and this is the way it came about: We were advancing behind our own barrage when the shells commenced falling short, killing some of our men and wounding others. There was no communication by telephone with the batteries, so I volunteered to go back to Regimental and report what the artillerymen were doing.

The German line made a deep pocket to our left, so the shortest route to Regimental lay across an open field and straight through the German lines. Captain Matlock said I'd never be able to make it through alive, but I thought I could do it, all right, and in ten minutes after I had started, I was at Regimental Headquarters giving them the dope.

After war was over I returned to my old job with

the General Hardware Company and I've been there ever since. In my home town people point me out to strangers and say, "You'd never believe that fellow had a hat full of medals, would you?" And the strangers always say no, they never would.

PRIVATE WALTER WEBSTER

"IT was different when war was declared, and the band was playing in Jackson Park and there were pretty girls dressed in nurses' uniforms urging the men to enlist and fight for their country: it was all different then, and all very romantic. . . ." That's what I said to Effie's mother when she came to me about breaking the engagement.

"Effie will marry you, if you insist on it," her mother said. "She knows what you have suffered. We all know that. She'll go through with the wedding, if you want her to."

"All right—I want her to!" I said. "We made a bargain: she promised to marry me if I enlisted. I carried out my part of the contract. She's got to carry out hers."

Effie's mother spoke slowly, trying to pick words that wouldn't hurt my feelings. "Probably you don't quite realize how—how—you have changed," she said. "Effie is a high-strung, sensitive girl, and while we all realize you have been unfortunate, and cannot help your—your present appearance, still . . ."

"Go ahead and say it!" I said. "I've got a looking-glass. I know how I look with my face burned and twisted to one side. Don't worry," I said; "I know how I look, all right!"

"It isn't that at all, Walter," her mother said. . . . "We just want you to come to Effie, of your own accord, and release her from her promise."

"I won't do it," I said. "Not as long as I live."

Mrs. Williams got up and walked to the door. "You are very selfish, and very inconsiderate," she said.

I put my hand on her arm. "She'll get used to me after a while. She'll get so she won't even notice my face. I'll be so good to her, she'll have to love me again."

What a fool I was. I should have known Mrs. Williams was right. I shouldn't have gone through with it. I can see Effie's face now. I can see her face that night when we were alone in our room for the first time in that hotel in Cincinnati. How she trembled and covered her face with her hands because she couldn't bear to look at me. "I must get used to that," I kept thinking. "I must get used to it. . . ."

Then I came over to her, but I did not touch her. I got down on my knees and rested my face in her lap. . . . If she had only touched my head with her hand! If she had only spoken one word of understanding! . . . But she didn't. She closed her eyes and pulled away. I could feel the muscles in her legs rigid with disgust.

"If you touch me, I'll vomit," she said.

PRIVATE SYLVESTER KEITH

I CAME out sullen and resentful, determined that such a thing should never happen again. I felt that if people were made to understand the senseless horror of war, and could be shown the brutal and stupid facts, they would refuse to kill each other when a roomful of politicians decided for them that their honor had been violated. So I organized "The Society for the Prevention of War" and gathered around me fifty young and intelligent men, whose influence, I thought, would be important in the years to come. "People are not basically stupid or vicious," I thought, "they are only ignorant or ill informed. It's all a matter of enlightenment."

Every Thursday the group gathered at our meeting place. They asked innumerable questions concerning the proper way to hold a bayonet, and the best way to throw hand grenades. They were shocked at the idea of gas attacks on an extended front, and the brutality of liquid fire left them indignant and profane.

I was pleased with myself and proud of my pupils. I said: "I am planting in these fine young men such hatred of war that when the proper time comes they will stand up and tell the truth without fear or shame." But some one began organizing a company of National Guard in our town about that time and my disciples, anxious to protect their country from the horrors I had described, deserted my society and joined in a body.

PRIVATE LESLIE JOURDAN

AFTER the war was over I moved to Birmingham, Alabama, and invested in a paint factory the money that my father had left for the completion of my musical education. I met Grace Ellis and she married me. We own our own home and we have three fine, healthy children. We have enough money laid by in safe bonds to keep us comfortably for the remainder of our lives. All in all I have prospered beyond the average and Grace, who really loves me, has been happy.

I had almost forgotten that I had ever played the piano at all when one day I ran across Henry Olsen in the lobby of the Tutweiler Hotel. He told me that he was touring the principal cities of the South in a series of concerts, and that the critics had given him fine notices wherever he had been. Olsen and I had studied together in Paris, under Olivarria, back in 1916, when we were both kids.

Henry couldn't get over the fact that I'd given up playing the piano. I tried to get him off the subject but he kept coming back to it and reminding me how Olivarria (he's dead now) used to say that I had more ability than all his other pupils combined, and to predict that I was going to be the great virtuoso of my day.

I laughed and tried to change the subject again. I commenced telling him about the way I had prospered in the paint business, but he kept cross-examining me closely and bawling me out for having given up my music until finally I had to do it. I took my hands from my pockets and rested them quietly on his knee. My right hand is as good as it ever was, but shrapnel has wrecked the other one. Nothing remains of my left hand except an elongated thumb and two ragged teats of boneless flesh.

After that Henry and I talked about the paint business, and how I had prospered in it, until it was time for him to leave for his concert.

PRIVATE FREDERICK TERWILLIGER

ONE night when we were in a quiet sector near Verdun, Pig Iron Riggin broke me out to go on watch until daylight. When I got to my post, I stood on a firestep and stuck my head above the trench to get a breath of fresh air. I was still grumbling sleepily to myself, I remember, and I yawned just when I stuck my head up. At that moment I felt a sharp pain and my mouth was full of blood. A stray bullet had gone through both my cheeks without hitting my tongue or touching a single tooth.

The doctor back at Base One was certainly a fine man. I told him how it happened and he laughed and slapped his leg. "You know what I'm going to do for you, kid? I'm going to give you the prettiest pair of dimples in the army!" he said.

I got married not long after getting out of service. My wife likes a lot of company, so once or twice a week she asks in some of the neighbors to play bridge or just sit around and listen to the radio. One night she had Ernie and Flossie Brecker over and Flossie said: "It's a shame the Lord didn't give *me* those beautiful dimples, instead of Mr. Terwilliger."

Flossie Brecker has a long neck and pale blue eyes that pop out at you like a frog's, and suddenly I had a picture of her head coming up slowly out of a trench. Well, sir, I laughed so hearty I lost count of the cards and had to deal over. My wife said, "Don't pay any attention to Fred; you'll only make him act sillier! I wish I had dimples like that too."

PRIVATE COLIN WILTSEE

NOW if you boys will gather around closer so that we won't disturb the other classes, I'll tell you a very beautiful experience which was brought into my mind by to-day's golden text. . . . Herman Gladstone and Vincent Toof were "pals out there," as we used to say on the line. Herman, or "Hermie," as everybody called him affectionately, was very different from Vinnie Toof! Hermie, while having "a heart of gold," used bad words, and did a number of things that he should not have done, while Vinnie was deeply religious, and had the fine qualities which I have tried to implant in you boys. Hermie scoffed at patriotism or religion or any of the things we consider sacred: But Vinnie, suspecting a finer side to his "pal," determined to win him for God, in spite of himself. . . .

One day when we were in the trenches near St. Etienne, a shell fell where a group of soldiers were playing cards for money, among them being Hermie Gladstone. A fragment of the shell hit Hermie squarely, and it was easy to see that he would soon "stand before his Maker." Vinnie came at once, when he heard the news. He had a testament in his hand, and when he reached his pal, he knelt down beside him, and began to pray and plead with him to accept Christ for his personal savior. At first Hermie would not listen to him: there was only bitterness in his heart. He cursed and reviled and begged his comrades to make Vinnie go away; but as Vinnie continued to talk to him and to describe the unending torment of Hell fire into which God casts all sinners, Hermie's attitude changed, and he saw he should not regret giving his life for his country: he realized that he could make no nobler sacrifice. A feeling of peace came over Hermie. He repeated the words that Vinnie told him to say and accepted Christ there on the field of battle, dying a few minutes later in his mercy and love. . . . The other men stood with their hats off, and their heads bowed, watching the miracle of Herman Gladstone's conversion. There was not a dry eye among them; but it was fine, manly emotion, and they were not ashamed of their tears!

And now I see the superintendent has given the signal that the other classes are all through, but before we go into the Sunday-school room, I want you boys to think about the beautiful death of Hermie Gladstone. Some day *you* may be called upon to defend your country and your God! When that day comes, remember our lives belong not to ourselves, but to the Creator of the Universe and President Hoover, and that we must always obey their will without asking questions! . . .

PRIVATE ROY HOWARD

I MET Sadie when I was on leave in Baltimore, and Christ, how I fell for her! She had the sweetest way of doing things I ever seen, like kissing a man when he wasn't expecting it, or holding his face against her breast and running her fingers through his hair. She would laugh and say: "Can you hear my little heart beating all for you, Mr. Soldier Man?"

She didn't really expect me to marry her, but I done it just the same. It didn't seem right, otherwise; and besides I couldn't bear to think of her alone and unprotected. When I got back to camp, I made her an allotment of every nickel of my pay. I done it gladly; I loved her and wanted her to have it. The boys used to say I was tight, and that hurt more than not having any money to spend for cigarettes or pinard, but I took it all good-natured.

I wrote Sadie as regular as I could, and I heard once or twice from her, but when I was discharged I didn't know where she was. I tried to trace her through the allotment, but she had moved and I couldn't find her. All I could learn was what the landlady told me, and she said that Sadie had been living with a taxi driver and that she had spent my allotment money on him. She said Sadie was on the turf now, she thought. So I went back to my old job as a riveter, and tried to forget her.

Of course I'm human, just like the next man, so after a time I met a little Italian girl whose folks had thrown her out and who was up against it, good and plenty; and before long we were living together down on Bleecker Street. She wasn't sweet, the way Sadie was, but I liked her, and we got along without any quarreling. But I didn't like the idea of living with her that way: it made me feel sneaky, so I suggested one day that we get married. Well, Mary (her name was Mary) cried and kissed me and we got married.

We lived together three years as man and wife, and had two kids in that time, all open and above board, and then one day I met Sadie on Fourteenth Street. She was just as sweet and dainty as she used to be, although anybody could tell that she was a strumpet now. She recognized me at once and tried to beat it, but I stopped her and told her that there wasn't any hard feelings as far as I was concerned. We went in a drug store for a soda. I said: "I remember you don't like anything but chocolate," and she said, "Do you remember that, after all these years?" I laughed and said, "Oh, yes, I remember that."

Sadie told me where she was living, and asked me to

come around and see her some night. "Nothing like that," I said. "I'm married and living happily with my wife. It wouldn't be right to have anything to do with street walkers now." Sadie reached out and patted my hand in her old sweet way. There were tears in her eyes. "That's right," she said. Then she asked me about Mary. She hoped that I'd married a good girl who would make me happy. She wanted to know where I was living, and I told her, and she wrote down the address on the inside of a match box. Then she squeezed my hand and wiped her eyes. I felt sorry for her; she looked so helpless and lonely as she walked away. I ran and caught up with her again and took her hand in mine. "If I can ever do anything for you, just let me know," I said. She shook her head.

That was Wednesday. On Friday morning when I was eating breakfast, two policemen came around and arrested me for bigamy; and Sadie sat on the witness stand crying into her handkerchief and sending me to prison for five years.

PRIVATE THEODORE IRVINE

IT seemed an unimportant flesh wound at first, but it wouldn't heal, and finally an infection of the bone set in. So they amputated my foot, hoping that would stop the infection, and for a time it seemed that it had. Then, when I had begun to hope, the bone began decaying again, and another operation was necessary. It went on and on that way; nothing could stop the rotting bone. By the end of the sixth year they had sawed my leg off in small pieces as far as the knee. I said: "When they unjoint the kneecap, the decay will stop!" But it broke out again, above the joint, and as the rot crept upward toward my thigh, the doctors kept sawing behind it. . . .

For ten years I have been like a side of beef on a butcher's block. I cannot remember, now, what freedom from pain is like. Everybody wonders at my willingness to stand the agony that I suffer every minute of the day and night. My mother and my wife cannot bear the sight of my suffering any more. Even the doctors cannot bear it: they leave overdoses of morphine near me, a mute hint which I shall not take.

I cannot get well, but I'm going to live as long as I

can. Just to lie here, breathing, conscious of life around me, is enough. Just to move my hands and look at them, thinking: "See, I am alive—I move my hands about," is enough. I'm going to live as long as I can and fight for my last breath. . . . Better to suffer the ultimate pains of hell than to achieve freedom in nothingness!

PRIVATE HOWARD VIRTUE

FOR a week I heard shells falling . . . nothing but shells falling . . . and exploding with blasts that rocked the walls of the dugout. Rocking the walls of the dugout . . . rattling the frosty duckboards. I became afraid that I would die before the meaning of my life was made clear. I thought: "If I use my head, I can get out of this!" I remembered a joke about a man who ran around picking up scraps of paper. After examining each scrap he would discard it quickly, and say, "No, that's not it!" So the doctors pronounced him mentally incompetent, and discharged him from the service. As they handed him his discharge paper, he looked it over carefully, to see that everything was in order. Then he smiled at the doctor triumphantly, and said, *"That's* it, all right!" "I'll do the same thing," I said; "my life is too valuable to be wasted on a battle-field." I crawled out over the side of the trench and commenced picking up dead leaves, talking rapidly to myself all the time. Sergeant Donohoe came out after me and coaxed me back to our lines again.

Back at the hospital, I was afraid those smart doctors would see through my ruse, but I fooled them, too. I was transferred to the United States, and later committed to this madhouse. Here's the irony of the situation: I cannot obtain my freedom, although I'm as sane as any man alive.

You are a fair man, let me ask you a question: How can I spread the glory of my cousin, Jesus, and how can I baptize him in the River Jordan from this place where my limbs are shackled? How can I thunder the incestuousness of Herodias, or how submit, at last, when that wanton, Salome, completes my destiny . . . shaking her loins for the gift of my head? How can I do these things when my words die flatly against the padding of my cell?

Cymbals clashing and spears and soldiers cursing and casting lots and blood running in rivers from the poles destroying life and creating life. . . . Rocking! . . . Rocking! . . . And white breasts rosy tipped walking beautifully over ruin and always shells falling . . . nothing but shells falling . . . and exploding with blasts that rock the walls of the dugout. . . . And me crying in the wilderness. . . . Crying with nobody to heed me. . . .

I have told them over and over why it is necessary that I be released from this place, but the guards only stare at me and chew gum rhythmically with slow, maddening jaws.

PRIVATE LESLIE YAWFITZ

AFTER supper I clear the table and wash the dishes, while my sister sits in a chair and tells me about her work at the office, or reads the morning paper out loud. One night she came on an item about the French Academy honoring the German scientist, Einstein, and conferring some sort of an honorary degree upon him. There were a lot of speeches made about the healing of old wounds, hands across the border, mutual trust and confidence, misunderstandings, etc. There was a picture of the ceremony, and my sister described that also.

"If it was a mistake and a misunderstanding all the way round, what was the sense of fighting at all?" I asked. I put down the dish cloth and felt my way to the table.

My sister sighed, as if she were very tired, but she did not answer me.

"Since they're all apologizing and being so God-damned polite to each other," I continued, "I think somebody should write me a note on pink stationery as follows: 'Dear Mr. Yawfitz: Please pardon us for having shot out your eyes. It was all a mistake. Do you mind, awfully?' "

"Don't get bitter again, Leslie," said my sister.

"I know," I said. "I know."

"Don't get bitter again, Leslie. Please don't get bitter."

Then I went back to the sink and finished wiping the dishes.

PRIVATE MANUEL BURT

I REMEMBER it as clearly as if it had happened yesterday, and not three years ago. The date was October 2nd, 1918, and my company was lying in reserve, not far from a shelled town, having come up to the line the night before, and dug in. A little before daybreak Sergeant Howie came over to the hole where Clarence Foster and I were sleeping, and began hitting my feet with the butt of his rifle. I turned over and sat up, and when the sergeant saw who I was, he seemed disappointed.

"I'm looking for O'Brien," he said; "Lieutenant Fairbrother wants to send some reports back to Regimental." Then he added: "By God! you can never find that bugler when you want him. . . ."

The sky was still dark, but toward the east it was getting a little gray. Corporal Foster woke up, then, and began to rub his eyes. He started to speak, but changed his mind. He turned on his belly, folded his arms under him for a pillow, and went back to sleep. I lay back, too, but a few seconds later the sergeant began tapping my hobnails again. "Come on, get out of there!" he said. . . . "Come on! You'll do!"

I stood up and began to curse the outfit, but Howie did not pay any attention to me. "Come on, Burt!" he said again. "The Lieutenant's waiting. . . . Come on: get going!" I got up, then, and followed the sergeant back to an old barn where Lieutenant Fairbrother and Pat Boss, the top sergeant, were waiting. The top handed me the reports and told me what to do. "You better have your rifle loaded and unlocked," he said; "there's not any line through the woods, and you might run into a German patrol."

"All right," I said.

"You'd better fix your bayonet, too," said Lieutenant Fairbrother. Then he said: "I've told you men time and time again to keep bayonets fixed when you're on the line. . . . I've told you over and over! . . ." His voice was high and nervous, as if he were going to beat in the field desk with his open palms.

I took out my bayonet and fixed it. "Yes, sir," I said.

When I came out, the sky was getting grayer, but it was still not light enough to be seen, so I walked through an old field, pitted with shell holes and grown over with weeds, until I reached the Somme-Py road, but I kept my eyes and ears open. Later on I cut off from the road, and through the woods, and I walked more cautiously. I was beginning to feel better. I remember thinking that if I had a cup of hot coffee, I'd be all right. It was light before I knew it; even among the trees a dim, gray light filtered. It was lonely and quiet in the wood and I felt cut off from everything and entirely alone. Pretty soon I found a path which ran in the direction I was going, and was following it, thinking about a good many things, when I turned a bend, and there, to one side of the path, was a young German soldier. He was sitting with his back to a tree, eating a piece of brown bread. I stood for a few minutes watching him. The bread kept crumbling in his hands, and he would lean forward and pick up the pieces which had fallen onto the ground. I noticed that he didn't have a rifle with him, but he carried side arms. I stood there, not knowing what to do. At first I thought I'd tiptoe back around the bend, and cut through the woods to the right, but that looked as if I were yellow.

While I stood there fingering my rifle, the German turned and saw me watching him. He sat staring at me, as if paralyzed, his hand, with a crumb of bread in it, half raised to his lips. He had brown eyes, I noticed, and golden brown skin, almost the color of an orange. His lips were full, and very red, and he was trying to grow a mustache. It was dark brown, as fine as corn-silk, but it hadn't come out evenly on his lip. Presently he got up and we stood looking at each other for what seemed a long time, as if neither of us could make up our minds what to do.

Then I remembered what they had told us in training

camp about Germans, and I began to get sore at him. I could see that he was getting sore, too. Suddenly he dropped his bread among the leaves and reached for his pistol, and at the same moment I raised my rifle he raised his pistol, but I was the one who fired first. I kept thinking: "Does he think he owns this path? Does he think he can make me sneak off through the woods, as if I were afraid of him? . . ."

The German had jumped behind a tree and was emptying his clip at me. His bullets were coming close, knocking off bark above my head. Then, when he had no more bullets left, he turned and tried to run through the woods, and I dropped to my knees, took careful aim and got him between the shoulder blades. He fell on his face and lay flat, got up and staggered, and turned his face toward me. His face was frightened and his eyes were twitching. I gave him the last bullet I had and he fell once more. He tried to get up again, and rush me with a trench knife, but I ran over to him and when he raised his chin up, I let him have my bayonet. I caught him under the chin and the bayonet went through the roof of his mouth and into his brain. He grunted once, and was dead before he touched the ground again.

I stood there pulling at the bayonet, but it wouldn't come out of him. I put my hobnailed shoe in his face and tugged at the bayonet, but my foot kept slipping

across his face, scraping the flesh away. Finally I un-
snapped the bayonet from my rifle. When I got it off, I
began to run down the path as fast as I could. I reached
the edge of the wood and hid in some underbrush until
I quit trembling. When I was quieter, I delivered the
reports to Regimental and told the runners sitting there
about the German I had killed in the woods. Everybody
got excited and they made me tell it over and over.
Coming back I didn't want to pass him where he lay
across the path, but I thought: "I'm in no way to blame
for this. He'd have killed me, if I hadn't got him first."

Again I tried to pull my bayonet out of him, but I
couldn't put my foot in his face any more. As I stood
there, I began to feel exhilarated and to laugh. "Well,
there's one Heinie who won't do any more harm," I
said. Then I took a ring off his finger for a souvenir.
I put it on my own finger and kept turning it around.
. . . "This is a ring off the first man I ever killed," I
said, as if I were speaking to an audience. . . . But before I got back to the line, I took the ring off and threw
it into the underbrush. . . . "I shouldn't have put on
his ring," I thought; "that will tie us together forever."

I remember all this happened on October 2nd, because we attacked the next day, and that was October
3rd, according to the official records. I kept thinking
about that soldier lying across the path with my bayonet
in him, and I talked it over one day with Rufe Yeo-

mans. He said there was no reason to blame myself. All the boys I talked to about it said the same thing. And so I forgot all about that German boy. It was only after the war was over, and I was demobilized, that I began thinking of him again. He came very gradually. At first I had a feeling that the ring I had taken was still on my finger, and I couldn't get it off. I would wake up at night tugging at my finger. Then I would feel ashamed because I was frightened, and I would lie back again and try to go to sleep. I had dreams about him, finally, in which I saw his face. And then one night, when I was fully awake, I knew that he was in the room with me, although I could not see him. I lay in the room knowing that he was there. "He'll go away again, if I'm quiet," I thought; "I've nothing to reproach myself with. He'll go away of his own accord." But the German wouldn't go away. It got so that he was with me in the daytime, too. He was with me when I woke in the morning. He went with me to work. He followed me everywhere. I couldn't do my work any more, and I lost my job. Then I rented a small room on Front Street where nobody knew me. I changed my name, thinking I could hide from him, but I couldn't. He found me that first night, and came into the small room when I opened the door.

When I knew that he was there, I lay back in my bed and cried. I knew it was no use fighting him any longer. There was no use running away. Until then I had not seen him, when I was awake, but I saw him that night. He came suddenly out of space and stood at the foot of my bed, and looked at me. I could see the marks on his face which my hobnails had made. My bayonet was still sticking under his chin, driven in so far that the hilt hardly touched his chest. Then he spoke to me: "Take this bayonet out of my brain."

I said: "I would take it out, if I could, but I cannot: It is driven in too deeply." Then he handed me the ring that I had thrown away. "Wear my ring!" he said. "Put it on your finger." I held out my hand and he slipped the ring on my finger. "Wear it forever," he said; "Wear it forever and ever!"

My throat was dry and my heart was pumping rapidly. I put trembling hands over my eyes and closed them tight, but I could not shut him out. He stood waiting beside my bed, and would not go away. He spoke again, finally, his voice puzzled and gentle:

"When I looked up that morning and saw you standing in the path, my first thought was to come over to you and offer you a piece of my bread. I wanted to ask you questions about America. There were many things we could have talked about. You could have told me about your home, and I could have told you about mine. We could have gone through the woods looking for birds' nests, laughing and talking together. Then, when we knew each other better, I would have shown you a picture of my sweetheart and read you sentences from her letters." He stopped talking and looked at me: "Why didn't I do what I wanted to?" he asked slowly . . .

"I don't know!" I said.

I sat up against the back of my bed, but I could not look into his eyes. He stood silent and presently I began to speak again: "I saw you eating your bread before you saw me. Before you turned around, I smiled at you, because you reminded me so much of a boy from my home town who used to laugh a lot and tell jokes. His name was Arthur Cronin and we played together in our high school orchestra. He was trying to grow a mustache, too, but it wouldn't come out very well, and the girls kidded him about it. . . . At first I wanted to laugh and sit beside you and tell you that. . . ."

"Why didn't you do it?" he asked.

"I don't know," I said.

"Why did you kill me?" he asked sadly. "Why did you want to do that?"

"I wouldn't do it again!" I whispered. "Before God, I wouldn't!"

The German boy rolled his head from side to side; then he raised his arms and held them outward. . . . "All we know is that life is sweet and that it does not last long. Why should people be envious of each other? Why do we hate each other? Why can't we live at peace in a world that is so beautiful and so wide?"

I lay on my back and pressed my pillow over my mouth and beat at the bed with my weak hands. I could feel ice flowing from my heart toward my head and toward my feet. My hands were cold, too, and dripping with sweat, but my lips were parched and clung together. When I could stand it no longer, I jumped out of bed and stood in the dark room trembling, my body pressed against the wall. . . . "I don't know," I whispered; "I can't answer your questions. . . ."

Then somebody, who was not myself, came into my body and began to shout with my voice, beating upon the door with my hands. "I don't know! I don't know! I don't know!" he said over and over, his voice getting steadily louder.

PRIVATE COLIN URQUHART

I SAW much during my thirty years as a professional soldier, and I have watched the reactions of many men to pain, hunger and death, but all I have learned is that no two men react alike, and that no one man comes through the experience unchanged. I have never ceased to wonder at the thing we call human nature, with its times of beauty and its times of filthiness, or at the level of calm stupidity that lies in between the two.

I have no theories and no remedies to offer. All I know, surely, is that there should be a law, in the name of humanity, making mandatory the execution of every soldier who has served on the front and managed to escape death there. The passage of such a law is impossible, of course: For Christian people who pray in their churches for the destruction of their enemies, and glorify the barbarity of their soldiers in bronze—those very people would call the measure cruel and uncivilized, and rush to the polls to defeat it.

LIEUTENANT JAMES FAIRBROTHER

I WOULD be the last man in the world to deny the right of free speech, but these pacifist propagandists are making our nation a nation of cowards and milksops. They should be muzzled and placed where they belong. Let me tell you something, and I want you to think carefully over my words: Just so long as the United States continues to lead the world in intelligence, wealth and culture, just so long will other nations envy our happiness and fear our prosperity. . . . You've got to look at it that way, whether you want to, or not! . . .

Why do you think Italy is training an army and preaching militarism? Open your eyes and look around you! Look at Japan! They're ready to spring at our throats at the drop of a hat! And England hates us! I repeat it, my friends: Our "cousins over the sea" hate us! . . . I tell you I know what I'm talking about! . . . "Brotherhood of man," indeed.—I'd laugh if the situation were not so fraught with danger.—Germany is not to be ignored, either.—How shortsighted we were to let them get on their feet again.—And France hasn't any love for us: anybody who saw her attitude toward

our own soldier boys—your sons and mine, gentlemen
—knows that! . . .

And I tell you my knowledge is not hearsay. I know
first hand what I'm talking about. I did my bit in the
last war. I enlisted when I might have stayed at home
and claimed exemption because of my wife and my little
children. But no man with a spark of patriotism or an
ounce of manhood would do a thing of that sort! . . .
And I say, again, my friends: I do not regret the foot I
lost crossing the Meuse on that terrible night of November 10th: I feel that I offered that foot on the altar of
my country's honor; and I am proud that you, my con-
stituents, have shown your confidence in me by reëlect-
ing me to represent your interests in the House of
Representatives. . . .

PRIVATE RUFUS YEOMANS

COME up some night and have dinner with us, the wife would be tickled to death to have the captain of my old company for dinner. She says that she feels she knows you already. No fooling!—She really does.—Let me know when you can come, so she can have a good dinner cooked up. You know how women are about those things, I guess. . . . Say, let's make a date right now. Let's make it next Thursday. Marlene Dietrich is on at the Bijou Theatre that night and we can take that in later, if we get tired of talking about the war. All right. Fine. Bring Mrs. Matlock, too, if she'll come. . . .

Now here's the way you get there: Take the ferry at Cortlandt Street that leaves at 5:04. That puts you in Jersey City in time to get the 5:18. Be sure to get the 5:18 instead of the 5:15 because the 5:18 is an express and don't stop this side of Westfield. Get off at Durwood, walk three blocks to the . . . Oh, never mind about that. You come as far as the station and I'll meet you in the Ford. Christ! but this is a break—running into you on the street this way!—Don't fail me now. I'll be looking for you. . . . Never mind! Let's talk about that Thursday. We'll have a long talk about old times.

PRIVATE SAM ZIEGLER

I WAS taking an automobile trip through the East with my wife and kids, that summer, when I decided to go see the old training camp again. My wife kicked like a steer, when I told her my plans, but finally we decided that she and the kids could visit her sister in Washington, and I would join them there the following Wednesday.

When I reached the camp, I went up to the commanding officer and told him who I was, and the name of my old outfit. He was very nice to me. He showed me a roster of the post and I looked it over, to see if any of the men I used to soldier with were stationed there. Finally I came to the name, Michael Riggin. . . . "Old Pig Iron Riggin!" I said.—"Well, what do you know about that?"

"Would you like to see him?" the commanding officer asked.

"Yes, sir," I said, "I surely would.—I'd like to talk to him about old times."

So the commanding officer sent out for Pig Iron and a little later we were walking about the camp together. I had an idea that I'd like to see the old bunk house we used to occupy before we went across, so Pig Iron got the keys and we went in. On the walls were a number of small silver plates, which marked where each man's bunk had been.

"That's a very good idea," I said. Then I stood there thinking. "As I remember it now, my bunk used to be over near the stove," I said. So we went over and looked at the wall, and sure enough there was a silver plate with my name on it. It gave me a funny feeling to be standing there looking at it. Then Pig Iron and I began to look at the other plates. . . .

"Frank Halligan," I said. . . . "Why, I hadn't thought of that old hard tail for years!—What's become of him, Pig Iron?"

"He's in the service, somewhere," said Riggin. "I don't know just where, though."

Pig Iron was also looking at the plates. "Rowland Geers, . . . was that the fellow who swam the Meuse when the bridge blew up?"

"Maybe so," I said; "I don't remember."

"I remember Carter Atlas," said Pig Iron, laughing. "He was the boy who threw his mess-gear away one night when we had rice again."

"I don't remember him," I said. "I don't seem to place him."

"John Cosley lost an arm," said Pig Iron, "or was that Ollie Teclaw?—Anyway, I remember putting a tourniquet on one of them, and whoever it was, he kept saying I was putting it on too tight.—You remember John Cosley, don't you?—A tall fellow with red hair . . ."

I stood there thinking, trying to bring up the faces of the men I used to soldier with, but I couldn't do it. I realized, then, that I would not have remembered the face of Riggin, himself, if I hadn't known who he was beforehand. I began to feel sad because it had all happened so long ago, and because I had forgotten so much. I was sorry that I had come to the camp at all. Pig Iron and I stood there looking at each other. We didn't have anything to talk about, after all. Then we locked the old building and went outside.

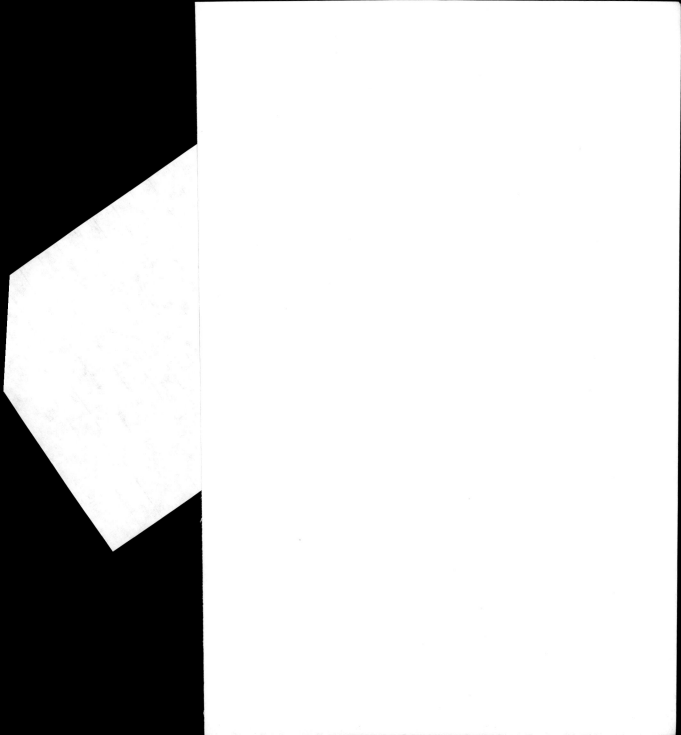

DATE DUE

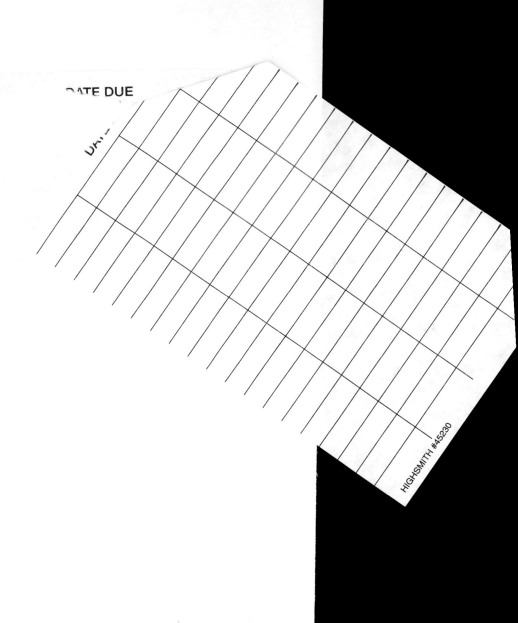

HIGHSMITH #45230